mixed bags

Other books by Melody Carlson:

Carter House Girls Series

Mixed Bags (Book One)
Stealing Bradford (Book Two)
Homecoming Queen (Book Three)
Viva Vermont! (Book Four)
Lost in Las Vegas (Book Five)
New York Debut (Book Six)
Spring Breakdown (Book Seven)
Last Dance (Book Eight)

Books for Teens

The Secret Life of Samantha McGregor series
Diary of a Teenage Girl series
TrueColors series
Notes from a Spinning Planet series
Degrees series
Piercing Proverbs
By Design series

Women's Fiction

These Boots Weren't Made for Walking
On This Day
An Irish Christmas
The Christmas Bus
Crystal Lies
Finding Alice
Three Days

Grace Chapel Inn Series, *including*

Hidden History
Ready to Wed
Back Home Again

carter house girls

mixed bags

melody carlson

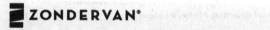

ZONDERVAN

Mixed Bags
Copyright © 2008 by Melody Carlson

This title is also available as a Zondervan ebook.
Visit www.zondervan.com/ebooks.

Requests for information should be addressed to:

Zondervan, 3900 *Sparks Dr. SE, Grand Rapids, Michigan* 49546

This edition: ISBN 978-0-310-74756-7

Library of Congress Cataloging-in-Publication Data

Carlson, Melody.
        Mixed bags / by Melody Carlson.
            p. cm. — (Carter House girls ; bk. 1)
        Summary: DJ's grandmother is a former fashion model who has restored an
    old mansion and turned it into a boarding house for rich teenaged girls who are
    interested in fashion, presenting DJ with a conflict between retaining her tomboy
    identity or changing her style, as she decides whether or not to try to fit in.
        ISBN 978-0-310-71488-0 (softcover)
            [1. Boardinghouses—Fiction. 2. Grandmothers—Fiction. 3. Peer pressure—
    Fiction. 4. Identity—Fiction. 5. Conduct of life—Fiction. 6. Interpersonal relations—
    Fiction. 7. Christian life—Fiction.] I. Title.
    PZ7.C216637Mix 2008
        [Fic]—dc22   2007033170

Editor: Barbara Scott
Interior design: Christine Orejuela-Winkelman
Art direction: Michelle Lenger

Printed in the United States of America

14 15 16 17 18 19 20 /DCI/ 20 19 18 17 16 15 14 13 12 11 10 9 8 7 6 5 4 3 2 1

mixed bags

mixed bags

1

mixed bags

"Desiree," called Inez as she knocked on the other side of the closed bedroom door. "Mrs. Carter wants to see you downstairs."

"The name is DJ."

"I'm sorry, but your grandmother has instructed me to call you *Desiree*."

DJ opened the door and looked down on the short and slightly overweight middle-aged housekeeper. "And *I* have instructed you to call me *DJ*."

Inez's dark eyes twinkled as she gave her a sly grin. "Yes, but it's your grandmother who pays my salary, *Desiree*. I take orders from Mrs. Carter. And she wants to see you downstairs in her office, *pronto*."

DJ grabbed her favorite Yankees ball cap and shoved it onto her head, pulling her scraggly looking blonde ponytail through the hole in the back of it.

"You're wearing that?" asked Inez with a frown. "You know what your grandmother says about—"

"Look," said DJ. "My grandmother might pay you to take orders from her, but I'm a free agent. Got that?"

Inez chuckled. "I got that. But you're the one who'll be getting it before too long, *Desiree*."

"*DJ*," she growled as she tromped loudly down the curving staircase. Why had she let Dad talk her into living with her grandmother for her last two years of high school? She'd only been here since last spring, late into the school year, but long enough to know that it was nearly unbearable. Boarding school would be better than this. At least she'd have a little privacy there and no one constantly riding her — telling her how to act, walk, look, and think. She wished there were some way, short of running away (which would be totally stupid), out of this uncomfortable arrangement.

"There you are," said Grandmother when DJ walked into the office. Her grandmother frowned at her ball cap and then pasted what appeared to be a very forced smile onto her collagen-injected lips. "I want you to meet a new resident." She made a graceful hand movement, motioning to where an attractive and somewhat familiar-looking Latina woman was sitting next to a fashionably dressed girl who seemed to be about DJ's age, but could probably pass for older. The girl was beautiful. Even with the scowl creasing her forehead, it was obvious that this girl was stunning. Her skin was darker than her mother's, latte-colored and creamy. Her long black hair curled softly around her face. She had high cheekbones and dramatic eyes.

DJ noticed her grandmother smiling her approval on this unhappy-looking girl. But the girl looked oblivious as she fiddled with the gold chain of what looked like an expensive designer bag. Not that DJ was an expert when it came to fashion. The woman stood politely, extending her hand to DJ.

"I'd like to present my granddaughter, Desiree Lane." Grandmother turned back to DJ now, the approval evaporating from her expression. "Desiree, this is Ms. Perez and her daughter Taylor."

DJ shook the woman's hand and mumbled, "Nice to meet you." But the unfriendly daughter just sat in the leather chair, one long leg elegantly crossed over the other, as she totally ignored everyone in the room.

Grandmother continued speaking to DJ, although DJ suspected this little speech was for Taylor's mother. "Ms. Perez and I first met when my magazine featured her for her illustrious music career. Her face graced our cover numerous times over the years. Perhaps you've heard of Eva Perez."

The woman smiled. "Or perhaps not," she said in a voice that was as smooth as honey. "According to my daughter, kids in your age group don't comprise even a minuscule part of my fan base."

DJ smiled at the woman now. "Actually, I have heard of you, Ms. Perez. My mom used to play your CDs. She was a serious Latin jazz fan."

"*Was?*" She frowned. "I hope her taste in music hasn't changed. I need all the fans I can get these days."

Grandmother cleared her throat. "Desiree's mother—my daughter—was killed in a car accident about a year ago."

"Oh, I'm so sorry."

DJ sort of nodded. She never knew how to react when people said they were sorry about the loss of her mother. It wasn't as if it were their fault.

"Desiree," said Grandmother, "Would you mind giving Taylor a tour of the house while I go over some business details with her mother?"

"No problem."

Grandmother's recently Botoxed forehead creased ever so slightly, and DJ knew that, once again, she had either said the wrong thing, used bad grammar, or was slumping like a "bag of potatoes." Nothing she did ever seemed right when it came to her grandmother. "And after the tour, perhaps you could show Taylor to her room."

"Which room?" asked DJ, feeling concerned. Sure, Taylor might be a perfectly nice person, even if a little snobbish, but DJ was not ready for a roommate just yet.

"The blue room, please. Inez has already taken some of Taylor's bags up for her. Thank you, Desiree."

Feeling dismissed as well as disapproved of, DJ led their reluctant new resident out to the foyer. "Well, you've probably already seen this." DJ waved her arm toward the elegant front entrance with its carved double doors and shining marble floor and Persian rug. She motioned toward the ornate oak staircase. "And that's where the bedrooms are, but we can see that later." She walked through to the dining room. "This is where we chow down." She pointed to the swinging doors. "The kitchen's back there, but the cook, Clara, can be a little witchy about trespassers." DJ snickered. "Besides, my grandmother does not want her girls to spend much time in the kitchen anyway."

"Like *that's* going to be a problem," said Taylor, the first words she'd spoken since meeting DJ.

"Huh?" said DJ.

"I don't imagine anyone is going to be exactly pigging out around here. I mean aren't we all supposed to become famous models or something?" asked Taylor as she examined a perfectly manicured thumbnail.

DJ frowned. "Well, my grandmother did edit one of the biggest fashion magazines in the world, but I don't think that means we're all going to become famous models. I know I'm not."

Taylor peered curiously at her. "Why not? You've got the height, the build, and you're not half bad looking ... well, other than the fact that you obviously have absolutely no style." She sort of laughed, but not with genuine humor. "But then you've got your grandmother to straighten that out for you."

DJ just shook her head. "I think my grandmother will give up on me pretty soon. Especially when the others get here. She'll have girls with more promise to set her sights on." At least that was what DJ was hoping.

"Has anyone else arrived?"

"Not yet." DJ continued the tour. "This is the library." She paused to allow Taylor to look inside the room and then moved on. "And that's the sunroom, or observatory, as Grandmother calls it." She laughed. "Hearing her talk about this house sometimes reminds me of playing Clue."

"What?"

"You know, the murder game, like where Colonel Mustard kills Mrs. Peacock with a wrench in the observatory."

"Oh, I never played that."

"Right ..." Then DJ showed Taylor the large living room, the most modern space in the house. Grandmother had put this room together shortly after deciding to take on her crazy venture. Above the fireplace hung a large flat-screen TV, which was connected to a state-of-the-art DVD and sound system. This was encircled by some comfortable pieces of leather furniture, pillows, and throws.

"Not bad," admitted Taylor.

"Welcome back to the twenty-first century."

"Do you have wireless here?"

"Yeah. I told Grandmother it was a necessity for school."

"Good."

"This house has been in our family for a long time," said DJ as she led Taylor up the stairs. "But no one has lived here for the past twenty years. My grandmother had it restored after she retired a couple of years ago." DJ didn't add that her grandmother had been forced to retire due to her age (a carefully guarded and mysterious number) or that this new business venture, boarding teen "debutantes," was to help supplement her retirement income. Those were strict family secrets and, despite DJ's angst in living here, she did have a sense of family loyalty—at least for the time being. She wasn't sure if she could control herself indefinitely.

DJ stopped at the second-floor landing. "The bedrooms are on this floor, and the third floor has a ballroom that would be perfect for volleyball, although Grandmother has made it clear that it's not *that* kind of ballroom." She led Taylor down the hall. "My bedroom is here," she pointed to the closed door. "And yours is right next door." She opened the door. "The blue room."

Taylor looked into the pale blue room and shook her head in a dismal way. "And is it true that I have to share this room with a perfect stranger?"

"Well, I don't know how perfect she'll be."

"Funny." Taylor rolled her eyes as she opened a door to one of the walk-in closets opposite the beds.

"I try."

"It's not as big as I expected."

"It's bigger than it looks," said DJ as she walked into the room and then pointed to a small alcove that led to the bathroom.

"Do I get any say in who becomes my roommate?"

"I guess you can take that up with my grandmother."

Taylor tossed her purse onto the bed closest to the bathroom and then kicked off her metallic-toned sandals. "These shoes might be Marc Jacobs, but they're killing me."

"So, you're really into this?" asked DJ. "The whole fashion thing?"

Taylor sat down on the bed, rubbing a foot. "There's nothing wrong with wanting to look good."

DJ felt the need to bite her tongue. Taylor was her grandmother's first official paying customer to arrive and participate in this crazy scheme. Far be it from DJ to rock Grandmother's boat. At least not just yet.

"Well, thanks for the tour," said Taylor in a bored voice. Then she went over to where a set of expensive-looking luggage was stacked in a corner. "Don't the servants around here know how to put things away properly?"

"Properly?" DJ shrugged.

Taylor picked up the top bag and laid it down on the bench at the foot of one of the beds and opened it.

"Don't you want to go down and tell your mom good-bye?" asked DJ as she moved toward the door.

Taylor laughed in a mean way. "And make her think she's doing me a favor by dumping me here? Not on your life."

"Here are some more bags for Miss Mitchell," said Inez as she lugged two large suitcases into the room, setting them by the door.

"Put them over there," commanded Taylor, pointing to the bench at the foot of the other bed. "And don't pile them on top of each other. This happens to be Louis Vuitton, you know."

DJ saw Inez make a face behind Taylor's back. But the truth was DJ didn't blame her. Inez might be a housekeeper, but she didn't deserve to be treated like a slave. Suddenly, DJ felt guilty for snapping at Inez earlier today. She smiled now, and Inez looked surprised and a little suspicious. Then DJ grabbed the largest bag, hoisted it onto the bench with a loud grunt, and Taylor turned around and gave her a dark scowl.

"Thank you," she snapped.

"Later," said DJ as she exited the room with Inez on her heels.

"Mrs. Carter wants to see you downstairs, Desiree," announced Inez when they were out on the landing.

"Again?" complained DJ. "What for?"

"Another girl just arrived. Your grandmother wants you to give her a tour too."

"What am I now?" asked DJ. "The official tour guide?"

"That sounds about right." Inez gave her a smirk.

DJ wasn't sure if she could stomach another fashion diva with an attitude problem, but on the other hand, she didn't want to risk another etiquette lecture from her grandmother either. Once again, she clomped down the stairs and made her appearance in the office, suppressing the urge to bow and say, "At your service, Madam."

"Eliza," gushed Grandmother, "This is my granddaughter, Desiree Lane. And Desiree, I'd like you to meet Eliza Wilton."

"It's a pleasure to meet you, Desiree."

DJ nodded. She could tell by how formal her grandmother was acting that Eliza Wilton must be someone really important—meaning extraordinarily wealthy—even more so than the Mitchells. And that's when she remembered her grandmother going on about "the Wilton fortune" this morning at breakfast. Of course, that must be Eliza's family.

"Nice to meet ya, Eliza," DJ said in a purposely casual tone. This girl was pretty too, but not like Taylor's dark and dramatic beauty. Eliza was a tall, slender, impeccably dressed, blue-eyed blonde. She wasn't exactly a Paris Hilton clone—and she didn't have a little dog as far as DJ could see — but there was a similarity, except that Eliza's face was a little softer looking, a little sweeter, but then looks could be deceiving.

DJ wondered if the Botox was starting to wear off, as her grandmother studied her with a furrowed brow, probably comparing her to Miss Perfect Eliza. Naturally, DJ would not measure up.

"Eliza is from Louisville," said Grandmother. "Her parents are presently residing in France, where her father just purchased a vineyard. But Eliza's grandmother and I are old friends. We went to college together. When she heard about what I was doing up here in Connecticut, she encouraged her daughter to send dear Eliza our way."

"Lucky Eliza," said DJ in a droll tone.

Eliza actually giggled. Then Grandmother cleared her throat. "Desiree will give you a tour of the house," she said. "And she'll show you to your room."

"Which is . . . ?" asked DJ.

"The *rose* room."

Of course, thought DJ as she led Eliza from the office. Next to her grandmother's suite, the rose room was probably the best room in the house. Naturally, someone as important as Eliza would be entitled to that. Not that DJ had wanted it. And perhaps her grandmother had actually offered it to her last month. DJ couldn't remember. But she had never been a flowery sort of girl, and she knew the rose wallpaper in there would've been giving her a serious migraine by now. Besides she liked her sunny yellow bedroom and, in her opinion, it had the best view in the house. On a clear day, you could actually glimpse a sliver of the Atlantic Ocean from her small bathroom window.

DJ started to do a repeat of her earlier tour, even using the same lines, until she realized that Eliza was actually interested.

"How old is this house?"

"Just over a hundred years," DJ told her. "It was built in 1891."

"It has a nice feel to it."

DJ considered this. "Yeah, I kinda thought that too, after I got used to it. To be honest, it seemed pretty big to me at first. But then you're probably used to big houses."

"I suppose. Not that I'm particularly fond of mansions."

"Why aren't you with your parents?" asked DJ. "In France?"

"They're concerned about things like politics and security," said Eliza as they exited the library. "In fact, they almost refused to let me come here."

"Why?"

"Oh, I think they felt I was safer in boarding school. If our grandmothers hadn't been such good friends, I'm sure they never would've agreed."

"So, you're happy to be here?" DJ studied Eliza's expression.

"Sure, aren't you?"

DJ frowned. "I don't know ... I guess."

"I think it'll be fun to go to a real high school, to just live like a normal girl, with other normal girls."

DJ tried not to look too shocked. "You think this is normal?"

Eliza laughed. "I guess I don't really know what normal is, but it's more normal that what I'm used to."

"But what about the whole fashion thing?" asked DJ. "I mean you must know about my grandmother's plans to turn us all into little debutantes. Are you into all that?"

"That's nothing new. Remember, I'm from the south. My family is obsessed with turning me into a lady. That was one

16

of the other reasons my parents agreed to this. I think they see the Carter House as some sort of finishing school."

Or some sort of reformatory school, thought DJ. Although she didn't say it out loud. Not yet, anyway.

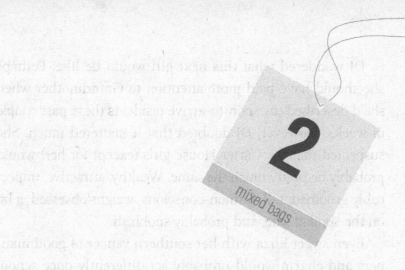

2

mixed bags

DJ was just feeling hopeful that life might return to normal. The house had been quiet for a couple of hours, and DJ had retreated to her room with an old Fitzgerald novel that she'd scavenged from the library. Then she was interrupted by a quiet tapping on her door. "Who is it?" she called out lazily.

"Desiree?" Inez poked her head inside DJ's room and then actually smiled in a sheepish sort of way. "Sorry to disturb you, but your grandmother is asleep, and we have another girl downstairs. Do you think you could show her around?"

DJ let out an exasperated sigh as she set the book aside and pried herself up from the padded window seat. She knew why Inez had come to her. She didn't want to risk her employer's wrath by interrupting her "sacred" afternoon nap. But weren't these girls Grandmother's problem, not DJ's? Still, after witnessing Taylor's rudeness to Inez earlier, DJ was resolved to treat the housekeeper with a bit more respect.

"I'm coming," she said as she shoved her feet into her flip-flops.

"She's in Mrs. Carter's office."

"Okay."

19

DJ wondered what this next girl would be like. Perhaps she should have paid more attention to Grandmother when she'd described the soon-to-arrive residents these past couple of weeks. However, DJ doubted that it mattered much. She suspected that the Carter House girls (except for her) would probably be pretty much the same. Wealthy, attractive, impeccably groomed, tall, fashion-conscious, weight-obsessed, a bit on the spoiled side, and probably snobbish.

Even sweet Eliza with her southern veneer of good manners and charm would probably act differently once school started. She and Taylor would probably both worm their ways into the "elite" clique—a group of snotty girls that held no attraction for DJ. The same girls who had pushed DJ (and kids like her) off to the sidelines—or worse, made fun of them.

DJ tried to block these miserable thoughts as she went into the office to meet the next Carter House girl. But, to her surprise, she found a petite, dark-skinned, black-haired girl sitting in one of the leather chairs. At first, DJ thought there must be a mistake. This girl not only didn't fit her Grandmother's model-criteria mold, but she looked really, really young. Like maybe twelve.

"Hello?" ventured DJ.

The girl stood now, holding her hands nervously in front of her. "Hello."

"I'm DJ," she told her. "My grandmother is Mrs. Carter, but she's taking a nap right now. Are you one of the new residents?"

"Yes. I'm Kriti Nahid," she said politely. "My mother is outside with the taxi and my bags. We wanted to be sure this was the right house. It seemed that no one was home."

DJ spotted Inez walking through the foyer just then. "Inez," she called, "Could you go and help ... uh, what was your last name again?"

"Nahid."

DJ nodded. "Could you help Mrs. Nahid with Kriti's bags?"

"Okay."

DJ turned back to the girl. She really wanted to ask how old she was, but a second glance told her that although Kriti was petite, she had curves and was most likely older than twelve. It was probably her Indian heritage (DJ's guess at her ethnicity) that made her so petite. Still, DJ wondered how her grandmother would react to this interesting twist. Or perhaps she was aware. Perhaps it had more to do with money and need.

Before long, an equally petite woman joined them, introducing herself as Mrs. Nahid, Kriti's mother. She was well dressed, and her jewelry looked expensive.

"We came by taxi from the city," she told DJ with a thick accent. "I do not want to let the driver leave yet. But his meter is running. I had wished to speak to Mrs. Carter before I depart."

DJ wasn't sure what to do now. "Uh, my grandmother is having her afternoon nap. I could wake her if you—"

"No, no, do not disturb her." Mrs. Nahid frowned. "Excuse me while I call my husband, please." Then she stepped out the door and made a call on her cell phone. Speaking rapidly in a foreign language (probably Hindi), she sounded very angry at whoever was on the other end.

"I am sorry," said Kriti, holding up her hands in a helpless way. "My parents are very protective of me."

DJ frowned. "And they let you come here?"

"We live in the city." Kriti frowned. "There is much crime. My parents worried for my welfare."

"Oh . . ."

"We have only been in America for seven years. My father's business is growing, but he needs to live nearby, in the city. They heard about the Carter House from friends. They felt I would be safer here."

"Right." DJ nodded. "That makes sense."

"I am sorry," said Mrs. Nahid now. "I just did not know what to do. The taxi was very expensive. It is a long way to the city. My husband said that it is acceptable to leave Kriti here now."

Mrs. Nahid had tears in her eyes. She reached over and grabbed Kriti by both arms, pulled her close, and hugged her tightly as she said something in Hindi to her. Kriti just nodded as her mother stroked her silky hair, but there were tears in her eyes too. Suddenly, DJ felt like an intruder. This was a private moment . . . a moment that DJ would give anything to have with her own mother again. She turned and looked away, but it seemed rude to just leave without excusing herself.

Finally, their tearful good-bye ended, and Mrs. Nahid apologized again. "I do not usually get this emotional."

"It's okay," said DJ. "I understand."

"I have met Mrs. Carter," continued Mrs. Nahid. "She seems a very responsible woman, and I know Kriti will be in good hands."

"Of course." DJ forced a smile as she wondered whether or not she should tell this unsuspecting woman the truth—or perhaps it was simply DJ's version of the truth. But in her opinion, her grandmother was not exactly the "responsible" woman that Mrs. Nahid seemed to assume that she was. And as far as "good hands," well, it probably depended on how one interpreted that.

"Can you have Mrs. Carter call me when she is awake?"

asked Mrs. Nahid. She handed DJ a business card. "She can call on my cell phone or at my home. Either is acceptable."

"Yes," said DJ. "Absolutely."

Mrs. Nahid said something else in Hindi to her daughter.

Kriti nodded, glancing at DJ. "Yes, Mother," she answered in English, probably for DJ's benefit. "I am absolutely fine. Please, just go ahead and leave. You better get going before you owe the taxi driver a thousand dollars."

Mrs. Nahid made a stiff smile and then nodded. "Yes. You are right." Then she thanked DJ and left.

"I can show you around," offered DJ as they left her grandmother's office, watching out the front window as the taxi drove away.

"Where should I put her things?" asked Inez as she came in the door with what must've been the last suitcase. She set it with the others, all mismatched and beat up and pretty unimpressive. For a moment DJ imagined Taylor's shocked reaction if these shabby looking bags were to end up in her room. It might be good for a laugh.

"I don't know," she told Inez. "Maybe just put them upstairs on the landing for now. Grandmother can tell you which room later."

DJ briefly considered offering to share her own room with Kriti. She knew that she would probably get stuck with a roommate eventually, and Kriti didn't seem too bad. Still, it was hard letting go of her privacy. And, as far as she knew, Grandmother's plan involved two girls per room, for a total of six girls. And she hadn't filled all the beds yet. Maybe she wouldn't.

Kriti remained pretty quiet during the tour. DJ hoped it wasn't because she was feeling bummed about this whole thing. DJ knew that it wasn't easy living away from your parents, but you get used to it, eventually. Finally they were finished and back in the foyer again. DJ wasn't sure what to do now. She wished her grandmother would come downstairs and take over. It was nearly four now. Usually Grandmother was done with her nap by now. Suddenly DJ felt irritated, like she was stuck babysitting this new girl. She didn't like it a bit. Was this how it was going to be? Did Grandmother assume that DJ was her slave girl?

"I can wait for Mrs. Carter in the library," offered Kriti, as if she sensed DJ's dilemma of having to entertain her.

"Do you like to read?" asked DJ as she led her back to the library.

"Oh, yes. I am a good reader."

"The books in here are kind of old, but there are some good ones too."

"I like old books," said Kriti. "I learned to read when I was three, and I have read literally thousands of books since then. My reading level has always been much higher than my age."

DJ nodded. This was Kriti's way of saying she was an "academic," and most likely she was proud of it. Probably a straight-A student too. Well, that was fine with DJ. Not that she cared too much about grades. And, really, it was preferable to being an elite snob who put everyone else down. Although DJ was well aware that some academics could be just as mean and superior as girls like Taylor. Whatever.

3

mixed bags

"So this is Kriti," said Grandmother, finally joining the two girls in the library. Her eyebrows lifted slightly when she took in the petite girl's stature. "Inez told me that you arrived during my nap. I am Mrs. Carter." She extended her hand.

Kriti shook her hand and smiled. "I'm pleased to meet you."

Grandmother nodded. "I see you've met my granddaughter, Desiree."

Kriti glanced at DJ curiously, probably wondering about her name, and then said, "Yes, she was very kind to show me around."

"And your mother has left?"

"Yes."

"I'm sorry I missed her. I hope she wasn't inconvenienced."

"She asked that you call her," said DJ, digging the slightly rumpled business card from her jeans pocket.

"Thank you."

"We didn't know which room Kriti was going to be in. Her things are —"

"Yes, I saw her things on the landing." Grandmother cleared her throat. "I will tell Inez to take them to the rose room."

DJ frowned. Grandmother was putting Kriti in with Eliza? That seemed a little odd, considering the way she had treated Eliza like royalty, simply because her family was so rich. But DJ said nothing. Mostly she was relieved that she was not being asked to share her room yet.

"Has Kriti met the other girls yet?"

DJ shook her head. "I think they're still in their rooms."

"I see," said Mrs. Carter.

DJ wanted to be in her room too. She was tired of playing handmaid to Grandmother. Let her deal with Kriti now. "I'm going upstairs to—"

"Oh, good," said Grandmother. "Since you're going upstairs, please take Kriti and introduce her to Eliza." She smiled at Kriti now. "You are a lucky girl to room with Eliza Wilton. She is a delightful young lady, and I'm sure you will find her to be a most congenial roommate."

Kriti nodded. "Thank you, Mrs. Carter. I look forward to meeting her."

So, knowing she was still stuck, DJ led Kriti up the stairs and then knocked on Eliza's door.

Eliza opened it with a cheerful, "Yes?"

DJ performed the introduction, trying to do it properly, politely. Probably more for Kriti's sake than for her grandmother. She suddenly felt a tiny bit sorry for Kriti. How would she feel about sharing a room with Miss Perfect?

Eliza smiled, but DJ thought it looked a little forced. "I'm pleased to meet you . . . , was it Christy?"

"*Kriti*," said DJ.

"Yes, well, I'm pleased to meet you, *Kriti*. That's an unusual name."

"It's Hindu."

Eliza nodded. "I see."

"Does your name have a meaning?" asked DJ, hoping to help Kriti feel a little more at ease.

"Yes, it means 'work of art.'" She looked down at her feet as if this embarrassed her.

"Isn't that lovely," said Eliza in a tone that sounded a bit saccharine to DJ's ears, even though she was still smiling.

DJ couldn't help but notice how completely different these two girls appeared. Kriti, short and dark, looked very insecure and totally out of her comfort zone. Meanwhile, Eliza, tall and blonde, seemed to be in perfect control. It was obvious who would be dominating this room. Already, it looked as if Eliza had made herself at home. Her things were spread everywhere.

"Hopefully you'll have room for Kriti in here," said DJ.

"Oh, I'm sorry," said Eliza as she began removing things from one of the beds. "I was unpacking and I got a little carried away."

"Bottega Veneta?" asked Kriti as she picked up Eliza's bag and politely set it on the other bed, which was now heaped high with clothes and things.

Eliza blinked. "Yes." Now she seemed to study Kriti's outfit more carefully. Although DJ couldn't see that it was anything too spectacular—just a pair of white capri pants, a black T-shirt, and platform sandals. Also, Kriti had a black bag slung over her shoulder. It was trimmed with some big brass rings and things. Eliza pointed to Kriti's bag. "Dolce & Gabbana?"

Kriti smiled shyly. "In a way."

Now Eliza looked suspicious. "A knockoff?"

Kriti nodded. "My father runs a knock-off business."

"No way!" Eliza leaned over and peered curiously at the bag. "It looks like the real thing."

"That's the point."

"But isn't that illegal?"

"No," said Kriti. "Not unless a design element is trade-marked." She pointed to one of the buckles on her purse. "For instance if this had the initials here, it could result in a law-suit. But my father is very careful about these things."

"How does he know?" asked DJ.

"He is very smart. And his brother is an attorney."

"So does he sell his knockoffs on the street?" asked Eliza in a slightly snooty tone.

"No, he is a legitimate businessman. He sells to stores, and they know the items are knockoffs. It's all in good fun since the customers know they're fakes. Besides it's profitable."

Eliza shook her head. "But it seems wrong."

"Why?" asked Kriti.

"Because, look at my bag. It's a real Bottega, and I paid $2,400 for it."

"Are you serious?" asked DJ. She stared at the purse and tried to figure out why it should possibly cost that much.

Eliza nodded. "I'm totally serious. And I'll bet Kriti's dad knocks them off for a fraction of that price. That's just wrong."

"Maybe it's wrong that you paid $2,400 for your bag," said Kriti. "Especially when you could've gotten one almost exactly like it for a tenth of the price."

DJ wasn't brilliant at math, but she knew that was $240. "That's still a lot of money for a purse," she said to both of them.

"Not when you want quality," said Kriti. "Sure, you can get

a knockoff in the city for, say, ten bucks, but it's a piece of junk that will fall apart in less than a week."

"That's true," said Eliza. "A friend of mine bought a Prada knockoff when she was on vacation, and it didn't even last her one day."

"In some ways, you get what you pay for," said Kriti. "Unless you pay too much."

Eliza did not look convinced. And DJ just felt confused. Her bag was a Fossil, and she thought it was perfectly fine, but she'd paid less than sixty bucks for it at Macy's. Of course, it was on sale. But still, it hadn't fallen apart, and she didn't exactly take good care of it.

"I don't get it," DJ admitted. "It's just a purse, for Pete's sake. Why does it have to cost so freaking much?"

"You're not into fashion, are you?" asked Eliza.

DJ shrugged. "Obviously."

"I noticed that too," said Kriti in a slightly superior tone. "I find that surprising—I mean, considering your grandmother."

DJ rolled her eyes now. "Thankfully, the fashion gene must've skipped over me."

"So, you don't care how you look?" persisted Eliza.

"I care." DJ frowned. "I just don't care as much as you do."

"Well, I don't care all that much either," said Kriti. Although DJ wasn't sure she believed her now. She might've earlier, before Kriti revealed her knowledge of big name designers. "I am much more into education than fashion. My parents researched the school we'll be attending here. Crescent High may be small, but it has a very impressive academic record." She smiled. "And I plan to graduate at the top of my class and then get a scholarship at one of the Ivy League schools. Harvard perhaps."

"What year are you?" asked Eliza.

"A junior."

"You look younger," said Eliza.

"Actually, I am. I was moved up a grade. Plus, I'm small. People always assume that means I'm younger. Still, I can't do anything about my size."

"No, of course not."

"Here are Miss Nahid's bags," announced Inez as she shoved the mismatched luggage into the room.

"Those are your bags?" said Eliza with open disapproval.

"I know," Kriti said. "They are pretty ugly. But it was what we had on hand. My father promised me a new set of Ralph Lauren knockoffs by Christmas. He said to throw these out as soon as I unpack."

Eliza laughed. "Good idea. Maybe we can have a bonfire out back."

Kriti unzipped a bag and began to remove her clothes, carefully laying them out across the bed. "I assume there are hangers," she said as she shook out a jacket.

"I'm already running short," said Eliza.

"What am I supposed to use?" asked Kriti.

"I don't know." Eliza frowned as she looked at all the items that were still piled on her bed.

"Just because you were in the room first doesn't mean you get to use my hangers," pointed out Kriti.

"Yes, I realize that." Eliza turned to DJ now. "The fact is I'm worried there's not enough closet space here. Does your grandmother have a plan for this? I could store some of my off-season things elsewhere."

"These closets do seem to be a little on the small side," observed Kriti.

"There's plenty of room in my closet," said DJ.

"That's not surprising," said Eliza a bit too smugly.

"This is an old house," said DJ, feeling slightly defensive now. "I don't think it was ever meant to have gigantic closets."

"Obviously," said Kriti.

"Can you please check with your grandma?" asked Eliza. "Find out what her plan is for storing our overflow of clothes."

"Right." DJ backed out of the room, eager to get away from what was starting to look more like a clothing boutique than a bedroom. "I'll let her know there's a problem."

Then, suddenly, as DJ was going down the stairs, she felt hopeful. Yes, there was a problem. Her grandmother had bitten off more than she could chew. Perhaps she should consider this and get out of this crazy scheme before it was too late. In fact, that was just what DJ intended to tell her. She would convince her to cut her losses and send everyone—maybe even DJ—packing.

She hunted around until she finally discovered her grandmother discussing the next week's menu with the cook. Rather, they were arguing about it.

"You can't possibly serve all those carbohydrates," said Grandmother. "That is six portions of carbs on Monday alone. The girls will all be as fat as pigs in a month."

"What do you have against carbohydrates?" said Clara in an angry voice. "This is food we're talking about, right? What am I supposed to fix?"

"I am simply saying that you have too many servings of things like potatoes, rice, and bread. You need more vegetables. And desserts should be things like fruit and gelato. Cakes and pies are out."

"Is this a boarding house or a prison?" demanded Clara.

Grandmother frowned down at the dumpy, middle-aged

woman. "It wouldn't hurt you to cut back on carbs yourself, Clara."

"Well!" Clara fumed.

"Excuse me," said DJ, thinking it was a good moment to interrupt.

"No more than two servings of carbs per day," Grandmother commanded Clara. Then she turned on her heel. "What do you want, Desiree?"

DJ quickly explained the need for more closet space, and her grandmother actually looked concerned, as if this had not occurred to her.

"And I'm wondering," continued DJ, feeling she was on a roll. "Maybe this isn't going to work out. I mean already Eliza and Kriti are fighting over closet space and—"

"They're fighting?" Her grandmother glanced back at Clara, who was probably listening. Then she took DJ by the elbow and guided her out of the kitchen, through the living room, and into her office, where she closed the door. "What are you saying? Are Eliza and Kriti really fighting?"

"Well, they haven't come to blows, but Eliza used most of the storage space, and Kriti doesn't have any hangers and—"

"I'll order more hangers."

"But the closets are too small," said DJ. "These girls came with a lot of stuff. Did you see how many bags Taylor had? I'll bet she's filled up every bit of space in the blue room by now."

"That shouldn't be such a problem."

"Why not?"

Her grandmother waved her hand. "Oh, I don't need to go into that just yet. But I can guarantee that her roommate won't be bringing a lot of things."

"Who is her roommate?"

"Rhiannon."

"Rhiannon? As in the girl who used to live next door? The one who used to clean the house for you?"

"Yes."

She's one of your residents?"

"I've made an arrangement of sorts."

"Don't tell me she's going to clean house for you in return for her room and board?"

"No, of course not."

DJ did not get this. All the other girls were about money and fashion. Rhiannon was a nice enough girl, and pretty too, but her mom was a little bit strange, not to mention a little bit broke since her divorce. And, due to financial problems, they had moved away about a month ago. DJ had actually been disappointed to see them go.

"So, how is it that Rhiannon is going to live here?" asked DJ. "What kind of arrangement?"

"If you must know, I am being charitable."

DJ was shocked. "Really?"

"Please, do not repeat it."

"Wow!"

"So, you see, Taylor shouldn't be too concerned over closet space."

"But why can't Rhiannon be my roommate?" demanded DJ. "I mean, unless I don't need a roommate. That'd be cool with me."

"No, I had other plans for you."

"What plans?"

"Well, I was waiting to surprise you, Desiree, but If you must know . . ."

"Who is it?" demanded DJ.

"Casey Atwood."

33

"Really?" DJ hadn't seen Casey since right after her mom had died, almost a year ago.

Her grandmother nodded. "Deborah called me just a week ago. It seems Casey got into some trouble in school last year."

"Casey got into trouble?" DJ had a hard time believing that. She had known Casey for as long as she could remember. In fact, Casey was the closest thing to a cousin that she'd ever had. Their mothers had been best friends since childhood and, although the Atwoods had lived a few hundred miles away in the Bay Area, their families had gotten together a lot. Even after DJ's parents divorced, they continued to be friends with the Atwoods. "What kind of trouble did Casey get into?" asked DJ.

"She got into the wrong crowd at school. Deborah was worried that Casey might turn to drugs, or worse."

"What's worse?"

Her grandmother just shrugged. "So, she is coming here."

"Is she a charity case too?"

"No, but she is getting a reduced rate. I call it my Friends and Family plan, and I do expect you to keep it quiet."

"Still, it's hard to imagine Casey getting into trouble. Her family has always been kind of religious. It seemed like they went to church about five times a week."

"I don't know about that, but I do know that Deborah seemed relieved that Casey was joining us, and she specifically asked that Casey room with you, Desiree. She thinks you will be a wholesome influence on her."

DJ chuckled. "And what do you think, Grandmother?"

"I think you need to lose that horrible ball cap, and we need to figure out how and where we'll get more closet space for everyone."

Despite her earlier plan of talking her grandmother out

of this whole thing, DJ experienced an unexpected pang of sympathy for the old woman. It was surprisingly sweet that she was letting Rhiannon come here. And having Casey as a roommate, well, that almost seemed too good to be true. And, even though she hadn't seen her for almost a year, she couldn't imagine how Casey could've gotten into trouble. Maybe her ultra-conservative parents had simply overreacted.

4

mixed bags

DJ was on her way to her room when she thought she smelled something burning. Worried that the house might be on fire, she began sniffing around. Finally, she determined the source was coming from the blue room, the room that Taylor had been assigned. DJ hadn't seen or heard a peep from Taylor since she'd taken her to that room nearly three hours ago. Hopefully, Taylor hadn't set herself on fire in protest of being placed in the Carter House against her will.

DJ knocked quietly on the door.

"Who is it?" barked Taylor.

"It's me, DJ. Are you okay?"

"I'm fine," she snapped.

"I smell smoke," said DJ. "Are you sure you're okay?"

Just then, the door burst open, and a hand reached out and grabbed DJ by the arm and jerked her into the room.

"What is your problem?" Taylor demanded as she leaned against the closed door and took a long drag from a partially smoked cigarette.

"You're smoking," observed DJ. The blue room, filled with smoke, looked even bluer now.

"You're brilliant."

"Thanks."

Taylor let out a long, slow puff of smoke. "Are you going to tell Grams on me?"

DJ coughed. "No, but it's not allowed, you know."

"I know."

"And you'll set off the smoke detector."

Taylor nodded over to the bed where what used to be a smoke detector was now in several parts, consisting of wires, white chunks of plastic, and a battery. "I don't think so."

"Why don't you smoke outside?"

"Because it's hot out there."

"Oh . . ."

"So, you're really not going to tell your grandma?"

"Do you want me to?"

"I don't really care. I figure I can get myself kicked out of here within a week if I try hard enough."

"You're really that opposed to being here?"

Taylor shrugged. "I don't know. I thought I was. But maybe I'll give it a try."

"Why don't you stay with your mom?"

Taylor sort of laughed as she snuffed out the cigarette in a soap dish that she'd confiscated from the bathroom. "She doesn't want me."

"Why?" asked DJ. "She seems like a nice lady."

"Oh, yeah, she's nice. She's just too wrapped up in her life, her career, and, more lately, her lover, to want to be bothered with a kid."

"Oh."

"What about you?"

"Huh?"

"What about your dad? Or is he dead too?"

38

"He's alive." DJ tried not to think too hard about her dad's lack of interest in her life, or how he'd shoved her off onto her grandmother last spring, resulting in this half-hatched plan to board potential models.

"Well, why aren't you living with him?" demanded Taylor.

"He remarried a while back. My parents were divorced before my mom died. My dad's new wife, Jan, well, she's younger, and she had twin girls about a year ago. I lived with them for a while, but Jan assumed I was the built-in babysitter, and when I didn't always agree, things got a little ugly."

"That sucks."

"Tell me about it."

Taylor shook out another cigarette and then held the pack out toward DJ. "Want one?"

DJ actually considered it but then shook her head. "I'm kind of into health. I do sports; I need a good set of lungs."

"Whatever."

"So, how about your dad?" asked DJ. "Why aren't you with him?"

"My dad . . ." Taylor paused with her lighter just inches from the tip. She snapped the lid on the lighter closed, returned the cigarette back to the package, and frowned. "Ever heard of the Betty Ford Clinic?"

"For alcoholics?"

"Bingo."

"Your dad is there?"

"For like the fifth time."

"I'm sorry."

"Anyway, when he's not at Betty's place, he's usually off doing something where a teenage kid doesn't exactly fit in. Not that I haven't tried. But my mom puts her foot down. Despite her selfishness with her own life, she still has this sense of parental responsibility where I'm concerned. Or so she says."

"My dad puts on that act too," admitted DJ.

Taylor went over to where she was still unpacking her bags and removed a purple dress that looked more like something you'd see on the red carpet than in a high school girl's closet. She hung it on a hanger and then held it up to herself and looked in the full-length mirror on the closet door.

"That's pretty," said DJ. "Was it for a special event?"

"A party."

"Must've been quite a party."

She nodded. "Oh, yeah."

DJ coughed again. The leftover cigarette smoke was starting to make her eyes burn. "Do you mind if I turn on the fan in your bathroom? To clear the air, you know?"

"Whatever."

DJ went and turned on the fan, noticing that the counter was filled with some very expensive-looking products and cosmetics. Taylor appeared to be pretty high maintenance—maybe even more so than Eliza. Still, other than her bad-girl attitude, which actually seemed to be improving slightly, she was rather interesting.

"Have you lived here very long?" Taylor asked as she put a fur-trimmed denim jacket on a hanger.

"I moved here last spring ... just at the end of the school year."

"So, did you go to the high school here?"

"For about a month."

"What'd you think of it?"

DJ shrugged. "It was different from where I'd gone in California."

"Different how?"

40

"Well, some things were the same—I mean, same kinds of cliques—but I guess what was different was trying to figure where I fit in. It's like everything had changed. I guess it's been changing ever since my mom died and I had to leave my old school. Starting over is kind of hard."

"Tell me about it." Taylor put the jacket into her nearly full closet and then went back to her pack of cigarettes. But this time before she lit one, she asked, "Do you mind?"

DJ shrugged again. "Maybe I could open a window? It's probably starting to cool off a little by now. The ocean breeze usually picks up around this time of day."

"Sure . . . whatever."

DJ cranked open the window and then sat down on the window seat next to it. The fresh air was still a little warmer than the air-conditioned house, but it smelled good.

"So, where did you used to fit in?" asked Taylor. "Like before your mom died? Were you popular? Or a jock? Or what?"

"Kind of in between. I did sports, but I was pretty much well-liked. I had a variety of friends. I was happy."

"Happy in high school. That's something you don't hear every day."

"How about you? I mean, I'd think you'd be popular. I mean your mom's a celebrity, and you're really pretty."

"Well, it's not as simple as it seems. You see, where I went to school, almost everyone had parents who were either rich or famous or both, so it's not like I was anything special. As a result, the girls were totally into their looks. I mean, I can't believe how many had plastic surgery, boob implants, nose jobs, you name it. On top of that, you had to dress just so. Like everyday was this big fashion show. Really competitive, you know. A lot of pressure to look really hot."

DJ nodded like she understood, and on some levels she did,

41

but part of this made no sense. "But it seems like you would've fit in just fine." And DJ could easily imagine Taylor blending in with the snooty girls at Crescent Cove High — the kinds of girls that DJ not only disliked, but simply didn't get. Stuck-up girls were so pleased with themselves and their rich and pretty Barbie-doll-like existence — girls who still had a need to pick on others. Like why should they even care? You'd think they'd be happy just knowing that geeks, freaks, and jock girls were around, if only to make themselves look better. What was the point in torturing the less fortunate? DJ realized she was getting lost in her own thoughts just now. "I mean, you'll probably be really popular at this high school." Okay, now that sounded totally lame.

"Maybe. It's hard to tell. Popularity is based on a lot of things, including conformity. And to be honest, that just doesn't interest me much. There are some games I don't like to play. I'd rather be myself; like you can take me or leave me."

DJ was feeling slightly hopeful now. Maybe she had misjudged Taylor. Maybe there was more to Taylor than appearance. "I don't like playing games either," she admitted. "Well, other than sports. But I guess I'm not exactly a conformer either. In fact, I'm more of an outsider."

"Well, I'm not saying I didn't have my own group of friends," Taylor said quickly, like she wanted to establish the fact that she wasn't a loser. "And I could mostly trust them, but not always. Part of the problem is that guys tend to like me. So I dated a lot, and sometimes that got messy with some girls, the ones who get jealous. You know what I'm saying?" Taylor peered curiously at her.

DJ nodded like she knew, but the truth was she didn't. Other than her friend Conner, who she'd shoot baskets with occasionally, she was pretty clueless when it came to the whole boyfriend thing. However, she was not about to admit that to anyone!

"Consequently, there were a few jealous girls at my school. You know, the kind of girls who think they're better than everyone else and want everyone to know it. The kind who like to make others miserable."

"So, it's universal."

"Yeah, and the dad of one of those girls practically owned Universal."

"You mean the movie company?"

Taylor nodded. "He didn't really own it, but the girl acted like he did. And when I started going out with her ex-boyfriend, you'd think I'd committed a felony. And this girl, because of her place on the social ladder, well, she made my life pretty miserable."

"Oh ..." DJ felt like she was in over her head now. Sure, Taylor had problems, but they were a totally different set of problems than what DJ had experienced.

"So, in some ways, it was a relief to leave."

"Well, you probably won't have to deal with anything quite like that here," DJ assured her, although she wasn't entirely sure about that herself.

She sighed. "Yeah, I guess it could be interesting."

"I mean there are definitely some families with money in this town — old money, as my grandmother would say. Like that's somehow superior. So there are a few girls at Crescent who can be a pain."

"You'll have to give me the lowdown on them before school starts."

"Speaking of girls, have you met any of the others yet? Two more just arrived this afternoon."

"No, I've been lying low." She pointed to the nearly full

closet. "And I've been freaking over the idea of having a roommate in here. There's a serious lack of storage in this place. But I'm thinking first come, first serve. My roomie is going to be in for a big surprise when she finds out she only has one tiny drawer for her stuff."

"You're not the only one with closet problems. My grandmother is trying to figure out some additional storage solutions. But, besides that, your roommate won't be bringing a lot of stuff with her."

"You already know my roommate?"

"Not really well. But she used to live next door to us. She's actually really nice. Her name is Rhiannon."

"Rhiannon." Taylor nodded. "I like that."

"And she's a really unique person. Really artistic and creative."

Taylor seemed pleased. "I like that too. What does she look like?"

"She actually sort of fits her name. It's Irish, you know, and she's got this mop of curly hair that's this great shade of auburn. The weird thing is that she doesn't like her hair at all. She was talking about dying it black. But I think it's really pretty as it is."

"We're never happy with our looks, are we?"

This surprised DJ. "I'd think you'd be happy."

Taylor laughed and then took a long drag. "Are you kidding? Don't you know that girls like me dream about being a blue-eyed blonde?" She shook her cigarette at DJ. "There were times I would've killed to have your hair. Is that your natural color?"

DJ reached back to where her ponytail was hanging down from her ball cap. She examined the end of it, which was fairly light, although that was deceiving. "It's natural, in a way," she said. "I used to do swim team, and the chlorine bleached it out. That and the sun and I could sort of pass as an almost blonde. Not that I wanted to." She pulled off her ball cap. "See, it's a lot darker at the roots."

"You should get it highlighted."

"That's what my grandmother keeps saying."

"Why don't you?"

She shrugged. "I don't know. Rebellious I guess."

Taylor smiled. "That's a weird way to rebel."

"Speaking of blondes," said DJ. "We have another one in the house." Then she told Taylor a little about Eliza and Kriti, including the discussion about designer bags and knockoffs.

"Seriously? Kriti's family makes *good* knockoffs?"

"Apparently. I'm not an expert. But I think Eliza is. Her parents are really wealthy, and she said she paid $2,400 for a Bogata Vendetta or something like that."

Taylor laughed. "You mean Bottega Veneta?"

"I guess . . ."

"Wow, she has one of those? Her parents must be loaded."

"Pretty much so."

"What's she like? This Eliza Rich Girl, I mean."

"She's okay, I guess. I mean I don't think she's a snob exactly. Or if she is, she covers it up with lots of southern charm." DJ imitated the southern accent. "She's from Louisville and just as cute as a bug in a rug."

Taylor rolled her eyes. "And the Indian girl, what's her name again?"

"Kriti. She seems okay too. She's an academic and doesn't care who knows it. Her goal is to graduate at the top of her class and get a fantastic college scholarship. And I guess she's a little into fashion too. At least she knows about fashion because of her parents' business."

Taylor's brows lifted. "Hey, I wonder if Kriti can get us knockoffs at a discount. There's a $2,000 bag that's killer. I've been dying to get my hands on one. Did Kriti happen to mention if her dad does Fendi knockoffs?"

"Fendi—shpendy! I expect this from my grandmother, but just how do you girls know all these crazy designer names anyway?" demanded DJ. "It sounds like you're speaking a foreign language to me."

"It's probably how you are with sports. You probably know all this jock-girl sports terminology that would be Greek to me." Taylor snickered. "Of course, it's not like I want to learn *that* language either. I would rather be dead than speak jock-eeze. But designers ... well, that's kind of important to a girl who wants to get ahead in this world."

DJ frowned. "You honestly think that knowing the names of designers is going to help you get ahead?"

"You know what they say: it's not *what* you know, but *who* you know."

"But it's not like you really *know* the designers. You just pay way too much money to buy junk that has their names on it."

Taylor laughed even louder now. "You really don't get it, do you, DJ?"

She just shook her head.

"And it cracks me up that you're so totally naïve. Man, you must give those snooty girls a nice big old target when you go around high school with your head up your—"

"Thanks a lot!" DJ stood now. She'd been thinking she liked Taylor, but suddenly she wasn't so sure. Taylor was probably just like the rest of the "elite" class girls—snotty and rude and mean.

"Sorry," said Taylor. She stopped laughing, but her eyes

46

were still twinkling as though she thought DJ was nothing but a great big joke. "But, hey, that's the best laugh I've had in ages. Thanks."

"At my expense."

"Toughen up, girl."

"I *am* tough," said DJ. "And I bet I could beat the snot out of you in any sport."

"Don't be so sure, Jock Girl."

"Yeah, right."

"Tennis?"

DJ narrowed her eyes. "You actually *know* how to play tennis?"

Taylor nodded. "You think you could beat me, Jock Girl?"

"You're on."

"Name the time and place," said Taylor.

"Tomorrow morning, the high school courts."

"It's a date."

5

mixed bags

"Sorry, I'm late," said Taylor as she breezed into the dining room. Everyone else was already seated, waiting for Taylor to join them.

"That's all right," said Grandmother with a stiff smile. She nodded to the empty chair next to DJ. "Please join us, Taylor."

"I thought we were expected to dress for dinner," said Taylor as she looked at DJ, who still had on jeans and a T-shirt. At least DJ had removed her ball cap—that should've made her grandmother happy.

Grandmother cleared her throat and narrowed her eyes on DJ, as if just noticing her apparel. "Yes, that is the goal, Taylor. Unfortunately, I am still training my granddaughter in the social graces. Perhaps you girls can be of assistance with Desiree."

"Speaking of social graces," said DJ, turning to glare at Taylor. "I thought we were supposed to be at dinner on time."

"Now, now," said Grandmother. "Let's not be unpleasant, girls. This is our first meal together. It should be a celebration. And to that end, I would like to make a toast." She stood, raising a wine glass that Clara (now wearing a uniform) had just filled with a red wine.

"Do we all get to make a toast?" said Taylor impertinently.

"Certainly," said Grandmother, obviously a little off guard.

"Where's our wine?" asked Taylor.

"Well, you girls are not … well, you're underage, my dear. Surely you do not expect me to serve you wine."

Taylor laughed with sarcasm. "No, I didn't think so."

"Now, back to my toast," said Grandmother. "I want to welcome you, the first of the Carter House girls. Here is to the wonderful year ahead of us, a year of growing and learning and becoming lovely ladies who are comfortable and able to conduct themselves with grace in any social situation that should arise." She smiled at the four girls, took a sip of wine, and sat down. "You may serve now, Clara."

As Clara served soup, Grandmother gave brief instructions on the proper way to eat soup, explaining that a lady always fills the spoon toward her.

"That's not how my dad eats soup," said Taylor. "He said you're supposed to push the spoon away from you."

"Yes, dear, but that's wrong. You see that is one of the ways the British could tell the difference between a distinguished gentleman and a lowly sailor."

"How's that?" asked DJ.

"A sailor would push the spoon away from him," explained Grandmother, "because he had been accustomed to eating soup on the high seas and it was safer to push the soup away from him in case the boat rocked. That way if the soup spilled it was less likely to soil his uniform. A gentleman, on the other hand, had no such concerns. He would simply dip his spoon toward him and gracefully consume his soup." Then she demonstrated.

50

"Without slurping, of course, and without putting the spoon into his mouth."

DJ watched the other girls around the table. It was hard to believe they weren't all laughing out loud at this totally ridiculous discourse on how to eat soup. Good grief, did her grandmother think they were a bunch of five-year-olds? But despite a couple of eye rolls, the other girls didn't seem too troubled by this idiocy. Even Taylor appeared to be applying the soup-eating tips to her own bowl. Or maybe they were all simply sucking up to her grandmother.

"I assume that you girls have all had a chance to get acquainted," said Grandmother.

"Well, you're assuming wrong," said DJ. "I'm pretty sure Taylor hasn't met anyone but me yet."

Taylor tossed DJ a warning glance. Perhaps she was worried that DJ was going to mention that she'd caught her smoking, although DJ had no intention to do so. At least not yet.

"Oh, my," said Grandmother. "I am terribly sorry, ladies. Let me properly introduce you all." And then she laboriously went through the tedious "proper" introductions.

"I've heard of your mother, Taylor," said Eliza. "My parents listen to her music sometimes, and I actually like it too. She reminds me of Norah Jones."

Taylor nodded. "Yeah, she gets that a lot. But the fact is my mom was singing long before Norah Jones was even born."

"Speaking of music," said Grandmother as she broke a piece of bread in half. "Can anyone tell me what is playing right now?"

The table got quiet, and the girls listened to what sounded like classical music. DJ knew that it was coming from an old stereo system set up in an antique cabinet in the foyer. Her grandmother had a fairly large collection of old vinyl records, everything from classical to jazz to pop.

"That is Vivaldi," said Kriti.

"Correct," said Grandmother happily.

"Do you know what the piece is called?" asked Kriti.

Grandmother looked slightly stumped and then her eyes lit up. "I believe it's 'Four Seasons.'"

"Correct," said Kriti. "But I mean which season is it?"

Now Grandmother was truly stumped. "Winter?"

"No," said Kriti. "Spring."

"Well, aren't you a clever little thing." Grandmother smiled at Kriti. "Do you play an instrument?"

"I used to play flute," admitted Kriti.

"And I hear that your dad makes designer knockoffs," said Taylor.

Grandmother cleared her throat. "We don't call them knockoffs, dear. Mr. Nahid manufactures quality products at reduced prices."

"Do you buy from him?" asked Taylor.

Grandmother looked slightly uncomfortable now. "Naturally, I do shop from many of the original designers, but I am not opposed to mixing in—very carefully I might add—a piece here or there that is a bit more affordable. I call that smart fashion."

Taylor pointed her butter knife at Kriti. "Can we buy things from your dad too? There's a Fendi bag I've been dying to—"

"Excuse me," said Grandmother. "Taylor, I must ask you not to utilize your cutlery as a pointing device."

"Oh, sorry." Taylor put her butter knife down on the table.

"And your butter knife goes like so," said Grandmother, setting her own knife crossways across the top of her bread plate to demonstrate.

DJ couldn't help but let out an exasperated sigh. Of course, this did not escape her grandmother's attention. "Desiree," she said, "do you have something to say?"

DJ just shook her head and rolled her eyes, another gesture that usually got a rise out of her grandmother.

"I can see we have our work cut out for us this year," said Grandmother. Then she turned to Eliza. "Eliza, dear, why don't you tell the girls a bit about what your parents are doing in southern France?"

So Eliza explained how her father had recently purchased an old vineyard and was now doing a painstaking restoration of the acreage as well as the home.

"Tell the girls how old the house is, Eliza."

"Parts of it are more than six hundred years old, but the latest additions are around a hundred years old."

"And the size?" persisted Grandmother.

"I'm not sure . . ." Eliza looked uneasy now, as if she were uncomfortable in the limelight. And DJ couldn't help but wonder if her grandmother wasn't exhibiting bad manners to talk about these things. Wasn't that a little like bragging? And hadn't her grandmother told her before that it was in bad taste? But so many of Grandmother's rules seemed bendable. Maybe it was what was called situational ethics.

"I heard the estate was quite large," said Grandmother. "I believe your father said the manor was close to thirty thousand square feet. That will be quite some undertaking. Goodness, this house is less than six thousand square feet, and it took me nearly two years to get it completely renovated."

"And you still didn't get the closets right," said DJ.

"Oh, yes, the closets," said Eliza. "Have you come up with a solution for storage, Mrs. Carter? Kriti and I are literally buried in clothes. We really do need an annex — perhaps a place where we can keep off-season garments."

"What exactly is an off-season garment?" asked DJ.

The girls laughed.

"Good grief, Desiree," said Grandmother with irritation. "Surely, you're not that ignorant."

"Well, I wear my clothes year round," said DJ indignantly. "Even swimsuits, like when I'm on the swim team, I still need them in the winter time. I guess I might have a warm parka or a sweater or two that could be packed away during the summer, but I don't really see the point. There's plenty of room in my closet."

"The point is, you don't understand fashion," said Taylor in a superior tone. "You think wearing the same frumpy jeans with a different colored T-shirt comprises a new outfit."

"I'm just not obsessed with clothes."

"*That* is an understatement," said Taylor.

DJ looked hopefully at Kriti now. "But you said you weren't that much into fashion either. You said you were more into education than fashion."

"I do believe education is vitally important, but I also believe that appearances make a difference in how the world receives us."

Grandmother actually clapped her hands now. "Well said, Kriti."

"I don't know," said Eliza, her expression softened toward DJ now. "I think it's admirable that DJ has enough confidence to go around dressed like that. It says that she is happy with herself."

"Or else she's just given up," said Taylor. "Kind of like those flip-flops she's wearing. Seriously, DJ, those things need to be put out of their misery."

The girls laughed again, and DJ felt like punching something or even someone, not that she'd ever been a violent person before, but maybe that was changing. Maybe DJ was changing. Instead of losing her temper, which she knew would accomplish nothing, she just stared daggers at her grandmother, who actually seemed rather oblivious as she chatted with the other girls, her darling little protégés, about closet space.

Why had this shallow, fashion-obsessed woman dragged DJ into her house of horrors? School hadn't even started yet, and DJ knew what lay ahead. If she thought last spring was bad, this was going to be much, much worse.

By the time dinner was nearly over — and DJ felt like a large stone had been wedged in the pit of her stomach — it seemed that Grandmother and her designer clones had resolved the clothing storage problem. DJ had been about to suggest an oversized dumpster in the backyard, but she controlled herself. Finally, after the raspberry gelato had been served, she felt it was safe to excuse herself, and — although Grandmother gave her a look that suggested otherwise — she made a hasty exit.

Instead of going up to her room, DJ headed straight out the front door. She wasn't sure where she was going, or even if she planned to come back, but she was so outta there! She walked and walked, finally finding herself down by the docks where she sat down on a pier post and stared out blankly at the surprisingly calm ocean. She wished she could hop aboard a boat and just float away. Any place would be better than here.

She felt hot tears trickling down her cheeks now, and she wasn't a girl who cried much. In fact, the last time she'd cried was when Mom died. Okay, she'd cried quite a bit then. But then she was done. She honestly didn't think she'd shed a tear since then, and she felt silly for crying now. At least no one was around to see it. Not that anyone would care. Not really. DJ felt more cut off and isolated than ever. It had been a lonely year, for sure, but she couldn't remember feeling quite this lost before.

What was wrong with her? Why couldn't she simply conform to be like Eliza and Taylor and even Kriti and just try to fit in a little? Wouldn't that be the easiest route? Besides, she knew that her grandmother's protégés would be the ones to turn heads when school began. They would be perfectly dressed, every hair in place, the kinds of girls that even the popular girls would be whispering about, envious of, and poking fun at. Of course, the Carter House girls would be an anomaly at Crescent Cove High: girls living in a boarding house with an old-fashioned diva who thought she could teach them manners. Talk about a big target. Still it might be safer being part of a big target than being isolated.

DJ took in a long deep breath and slowly exhaled. No, she thought, she would rather hang onto her integrity and be different. Even if it meant being picked on. She was who she was. Sure it wasn't much, but maybe that was all she had. Maybe it was better to hold onto it.

Besides, she reminded herself, Casey was coming. And Rhiannon. Two girls who were more like her. Maybe the three of them could join forces. Maybe they could even win Kriti or Eliza over to the "sensible" side. Taylor seemed a lost cause. Oh, she had been fun and interesting, if only briefly. But when it came right down to it, Taylor was out for one thing and one thing only—and that was Taylor.

"Hey," called a male voice from behind her.

DJ jumped so quickly that she almost fell off the pier post, which would've landed her in some pretty grungy-looking water down below the dock. Then she looked over her shoulder and saw that Conner was behind her.

"Hey, Conner," she said, hopping off the pier and hoping

that her tears had dried. No way was she going to reach up and wipe them.

"What's up?"

"Nothing."

"Did I scare you?"

She shrugged. "I guess you kind of startled me."

He grinned. "I thought maybe you were going to jump into the water, and then I'd have to make like the hero and rescue you."

"Yeah, right." She rolled her eyes. "Just so you know, I'm a good swimmer."

"I figured, but what if you hit your head on the way down?"

She frowned up at him. "Sounds like you have this all planned out."

"Nah, but a guy wants to be ready for anything. It was our Boy Scout motto, you know."

"You were a Boy Scout?"

"Yeah, for a couple of years before my dad took off. I quit after that."

"What about your stepdad? He seems cool."

He nodded. "Yeah, he actually encouraged me to get back into it, but I was too old by then. It was pretty uncool to be a Scout in middle school."

"So what are you up to?" asked DJ.

"Just hanging out. Man, it was hot today."

"Yeah, I pretty much hid out in the house all day."

"Wanna get a Coke?"

DJ was surprised by his invitation. So far she and Conner had only played a little basketball together and joked around. Asking her to get a Coke seemed like taking the relationship to a new level. She wasn't sure.

"You're not thirsty?" he persisted.

"Actually, I am," she admitted. "But I left the house so quickly that I didn't even grab a bag. I'm broke."

He laughed. "Hey, I was the one asking you. Why don't you let me handle the finances on this?"

She smiled now. "Sure, a Coke sounds good. Thanks."

6

mixed bags

DJ wondered if this was a date, as she and Conner walked toward town. *No,* she thought, *it's just hanging with a friend. A date is something that's prearranged, and the guy comes to your house and picks you up.* Still, it was the closest thing she'd had to a date. She partially blamed this on the fact that her mother had died when she was fifteen and, according to her mom, was still not old enough to date. Then, just as she'd gotten interested in a guy while living with her dad and Jan and the cantankerous twins, it had been time to relocate.

"So what have you been up to lately?" he asked as they walked down Main Street toward the Hammerhead Café—Conner's choice and a place DJ hadn't been to yet.

She told him about the new arrivals at Carter House. She tried to paint a light picture of the situation, but did let on that it was going to take some getting used to.

"Anyway," she said as they sat at one of the outside picnic tables covered in some slightly grimy oilcloth. "It felt a little crowded in there, and I just needed to get away."

"So what are they like?"

"Huh?" She studied his shaggy brown hair, noticing how

59

the sun had bleached the ends some, but it was actually a shade or two darker than her own. Still it was attractive in a beach-boy sort of way.

"The other girls I mean. What are they like?"

"Oh, well, I have to admit that they're really pretty. My grandmother probably wouldn't let a girl live there if she weren't pretty. Well, except me, and that's only because I'm family."

"You're pretty."

DJ laughed. "Yeah, right. But, thanks anyway."

"No, you really are." He leaned in as if to study her more closely. "I mean you're not a frilly kind of girl. Kind of what I'd call low maintenance."

"How would you even know what that was?"

"My sister Amy. She's in college now, and she might've calmed down some. But when she was at home, she was what I'd call really high maintenance. Seriously, she would not step out of the house if she hadn't washed, blown-dry, and styled her hair within an inch of its life. Then she had to put on these layers of makeup that took like an hour. After that, she'd try on about twenty things out of her closet until she had the perfect outfit. I swear that girl had to get up at four in the morning just to make it to school on time."

DJ laughed. "Yeah, I guess that is high maintenance."

"Which you obviously are not."

She frowned. "It's that obvious?"

"It's not a bad thing, DJ. I think it's pretty cool that you don't put a lot of time and fuss into your appearance."

"Kinda like one of the guys." She couldn't help but frown as she wondered what Conner's real perception of her might be.

But he just smiled. And his blue eyes sparkled in a way that she couldn't be sure was serious or not. "Yeah, except you're better to look at than a guy."

Thankfully, the waitress came to take their order just then.

"Want some fries too?" asked Conner.

She grinned. "Actually, that sounds pretty good. It was kind of hard to eat tonight with so much going on at the table. I just wanted to get out of there."

So he ordered a large side of fries and two Cokes. As a distraction from talking about looks, DJ asked if he planned to play fall soccer and when practices start. She was pretty sure he'd already told her, but it was a good way to move the conversation.

"Varsity practice started already," he told her. "For guys anyway. It started last week. I thought I mentioned it."

She nodded. "Maybe you did. Guess I'm kinda spacey with all the craziness going on at my house. Did I tell you that Rhiannon is going to live there?"

"Really? How'd that happen?"

"I guess her mom and my grandma worked something out."

"Rhiannon should be glad. She was pretty bummed about moving."

Then DJ told him about Rhiannon's roommate, Taylor, and her celebrity mother.

"I've heard that name," he said. "Cool. Someone almost famous."

DJ rolled her eyes.

"You don't like this Taylor girl very much, do you?"

"I thought I liked her. I mean not so much at first because she seemed kind of snotty. But then I hung with her awhile this afternoon—after I caught her smoking."

He chuckled. "Does your grandma know about that?"

"No."

"Good blackmail material."

"My grandmother probably wouldn't even believe me. I'm sure she thinks those girls are all perfect, and that I'm the loser of the bunch."

He frowned. "Why would she think that?"

"You haven't met my grandmother yet, have you?"

"I know she was somebody big in the fashion world. My mom and sister both told me that much. They were impressed."

"Yeah, people who are into fashion and all that nonsense are totally impressed. My grandmother likes to be surrounded by people who are impressed with her, and I'm just not. I mean who cares if she was a supermodel back in the Stone Age. In my opinion, fashion magazines only contribute to eating disorders and body-image problems. Who needs them?"

He nodded. "Okay, I get it now."

"So I'm like ..." she tried to think of a metaphor. "Like the odd girl out, I guess."

"That must be hard."

"Anyway, for a little while, I thought maybe I liked Taylor and maybe she had more going on than just surface stuff. Then it was like she totally turned on me. I can't even remember why exactly. I think it was mostly related to fashion ... like if I can't speak fashioneeze, or know the stupid names of the stupid designers, I'm not good enough to be her friend."

"That's pretty harsh."

"Yeah, but then I did something pretty stupid."

"What?"

So she told him about the tennis match, and he just laughed.

"Dumb, huh?" she said.

"Or it could be fun. Are you any good at tennis?"

"I'm okay."

He grinned. "Yeah, you probably are, DJ. I think you're just a natural at most sports."

She shrugged. "Maybe Taylor will forget about it."

Now the waitress returned with their order and, once again, DJ thanked Conner. Then she felt embarrassed, like maybe it was overkill, but this whole thing was still new to her. And she didn't want to seem unappreciative either. Conner seemed like a really nice guy; he seemed to get her. And sitting here, just having a normal conversation with a normal guy, was hugely reassuring. Maybe she wasn't such a hopeless loser after all.

"So how about you, DJ? Are you going to play soccer too?"

"Yeah, but you probably heard they aren't having fall soccer for girls this year. I guess there aren't enough schools in the area to play. But I'll play in the spring. In the meantime, I'll go out for volleyball. I didn't play last year, and it'll be fun to see if I still know how."

"I'm sure you'll be good at it," he said.

So as they occupied themselves by talking about sports, eating fries, and sipping on Cokes, DJ realized it was the most fun she'd had in days—maybe weeks or even months. And by the time they finished and were walking back toward their neighborhood, she felt almost hopeful. The sky was getting dusky blue and she could hear a woman's voice calling her kids to come inside and "get ready for bed."

"Thanks, Conner," she told him as they stopped in front of her grandmother's house. "I wasn't going to say anything, but I was feeling pretty bummed when I was down at the docks."

"I could tell."

She looked curiously at him. "You could?"

He nodded. "Yeah, I guess the waterworks kind of gave you away."

"Oh."

"See ya around then?" His eyes looked hopeful.

"Sure," she told him.

"Good luck . . . in the big tennis match, I mean."

She kind of laughed. "Yeah, thanks."

Her step felt a lot springier as she walked toward the house. The lights were on inside, and it almost looked cheerful in there. Still, she paused on the porch, unsure as to whether she was ready to go in or not.

"Big date tonight?"

DJ jumped to see the red glow of a cigarette burning in the shadows of the porch. "Taylor?"

"Who else?"

"I didn't see you."

"Who is he?"

"Who?"

"Your boyfriend."

"He's not my boyfriend."

"Yeah, whatever. What's his name?"

"Conner."

"And he's not your boyfriend."

"He's just a friend."

"He's cute."

DJ barely nodded. "I guess."

"And built too."

DJ just shrugged, acting as if she hadn't noticed, but the fact that Taylor had was somewhat irritating.

"One of your sports-jock friends?"

"Yeah, he's into sports."

"Like you?"

DJ put her hands on her hips now, taking a step closer to where Taylor was curled up like a cat in one of the wicker chairs, taking a slow drag on her cigarette, which made the end glow bright red. Obviously, she wasn't too concerned about whether anyone knew or not. Or maybe she wanted to get caught. DJ just glared at her without saying anything.

"What's your problem?" asked Taylor.

"Look, Taylor, I don't know why you've set your sights on me, but it's getting old, okay?"

"I don't have my sights set on *anyone*." Taylor let out a long puff of smoke. "Least of all you, *Desiree*."

"The name is DJ."

"Whatever."

"Fine." DJ turned to go into the house. There was no point in trying to connect with this infuriating girl. It seemed perfectly clear that Taylor had a chip the size of a Hummer on her shoulder. Probably because her celebrity mommy had dumped her here. But then what made Taylor's case any more special than DJ's? At least Taylor's parents were both still alive.

Just as DJ's hand reached the handle of the front door, Taylor called out, "Don't forget."

DJ looked back at her. "Forget *what?*"

"Our little tennis match. You promised to clean my clock, DJ. Or did you forget?"

"Don't worry. I didn't forget."

"But maybe you want to chicken out?"

"I am not a chicken."

"So you're still up for it then?"

"Of course."

"I invited Eliza and Kriti to come with us. They think it'll be a kick. We thought we'd go around ten. Eliza will drive us."

"Grandmother is letting her use the Mercedes?" Now this

really burned since her grandmother had barely let DJ use her car.

"Eliza has her own car."

"Where?"

"Here. It was delivered after dinner, right after you sneaked off." Taylor nodded toward the side of the house. "It's parked in back. Nice set of wheels too."

For some reason this aggravated DJ even more. Whether it was that Taylor was in the loop and DJ wasn't—or the fact that Eliza had her own car—but something about this whole thing just irked her. Even so, she forced a smile as she made a cheerful little wave. "See you in the morning, Taylor."

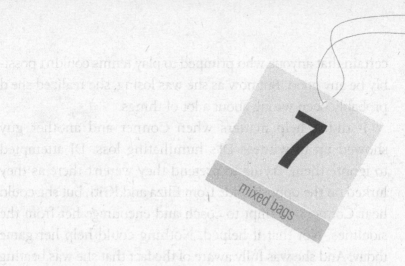

"That was out!" cried DJ as she shook her racket at Taylor.

"No way," said Taylor as she prepared to serve again. "It was totally in, Desiree."

"The name's DJ," she yelled. "And that serve was out!"

"Get ready," said Taylor. "I'm serving again."

"You're cheating!" yelled DJ.

Taylor paused with her racket still poised and ready to serve. She looked over to the sidelines where Eliza and Kriti were sitting, sipping their Starbucks. "What do you girls say?"

"Yeah," called DJ. "It was out, wasn't it?"

"Sorry, but Taylor's right," called Eliza, as if she thought she'd just been appointed line judge. "It was in."

Kriti nodded and held up a thumb. "In!"

"Out!" demanded DJ. She glared at Eliza and Kriti now. It was clear what was happening here; the fashion girls were aligning themselves against her. She wondered why she'd even agreed to this stupid tennis match in the first place. What was the point if Taylor already had everyone in her pocket?

DJ had assumed she had this game in the bag when Taylor came down to breakfast looking like Tennis Barbie. She felt certain that anyone who primped to play tennis couldn't possibly be any good. But now as she was losing, she realized she'd probably been wrong about a lot of things.

It didn't help matters when Conner and another guy showed up to witness DJ's humiliating loss. DJ attempted to ignore them, trying to pretend they weren't there as they lurked on the opposite side from Eliza and Kriti, but she could hear Conner's attempt to coach and encourage her from the sidelines. Not that it helped. Nothing could help her game today. And she was fully aware of the fact that she was beating herself as much as Taylor was winning this stupid match. Of course, that only made her madder.

Taylor was an average player. Okay, maybe even better than average. But DJ had totally psyched herself out right from the start when she'd allowed her anger and embarrassment to get the best of her over some close shots that she felt Taylor called unfairly. After that she was too rattled to focus much, and Taylor had her running all over the court just to return shots, many of which she missed. When it was all finished, DJ only had herself to blame — the worst way to lose.

"Nice game," said Taylor with a slight smirk as she reached over the net to shake DJ's hand.

DJ rolled her eyes. "Yeah, right. Back at you." She just wanted to get out of here, and the sooner the better. She actually considered making a run for it, but knew that would probably look totally lame.

"Hey, DJ," called Conner from where he and the other guy were now walking over to join the girls. "Too bad for you."

DJ sighed. "I messed up from the start," she said defensively. "After that it was all downhill." She adjusted her ball cap and then glanced over her shoulder and across the street, trying to think of a way to make a graceful exit.

Conner nodded, smiling at Taylor now. "Yeah, DJ's a great athlete. I think you just caught her on an off day." Then Conner kept looking at Taylor, gazing at her in a way that seemed to show she had gotten his attention ... and was keeping it. Taylor smiled back at him, as if she knew she had him. And DJ seethed.

"Oh, I'm sure that's the case," said Taylor in what seemed an overly seductive voice now, especially considering they were standing around on a public tennis court, drenched in sweat. At least DJ was drenched in sweat. Taylor still looked cool as a spring breeze.

"Are you going to introduce us to your friends?" Eliza asked DJ as she and Kriti came over to join the foursome.

DJ restrained herself from hitting Taylor, as she politely introduced her "new friends" to Conner, explaining how the girls were new in town but would be going to high school with them. She was so polite, especially considering how she felt, that she thought even her grandmother might be proud. Or not. She turned to Conner with a stiff smile.

"I don't think I've met your friend."

"This is Harry Green," said Conner casually. "Harry and his family are old-timers here in Crescent Cove. They go back ... like how far, Harry? To the Mayflower, or was it even before that?"

Harry shrugged and made a half smile. "Something like that."

"My family goes back to before the Revolution," said Eliza. She pushed her sunglasses up to reveal sparkling blue eyes as she smiled at Harry.

"Pleased to meet you," said Harry, his gaze fixed on her. "Welcome to Crescent Cove."

"Thank you," said Eliza. "From what I've seen, it's a pretty little town."

"It's okay," he said. "You sound like you're from the south."

She nodded. "Louisville."

"I've been there," said Harry. "I have some relatives, but Louisville is a whole lot bigger than our town. You think you can get used to a place like this?"

"I love that it's near the ocean," she said. "Not that I've seen much yet. I just got here yesterday."

"Maybe you need a tour guide," offered Harry. "Not that there's much to see, but if you're interested in a little tour, I'd be more than happy to show you around." He jerked his thumb over to where a blue Jeep Wrangler with its top down was parked nearby. "That's my ride there."

Then Eliza nodded in the opposite direction, where she'd parked her little white Porsche convertible, also with the top down. "I have wheels too."

Harry let out a low whistle. "Man, do you ever."

"Why don't we all head to the beach?" suggested Taylor.

"Great idea," said Conner. "Town's going to be crawling with tourists anyway, since it's Labor Day weekend and all."

"And the weather couldn't be better," said Eliza. "So nice that it cooled down after yesterday."

"And we've got a great spot on the beach," said Harry. "It's a place that only locals know about."

"Sounds good," said Eliza. She turned to Kriti. "You in?"

Kriti shrugged, as if she was unsure. "I don't know ..."

"Oh, come on," said Eliza. "It'll be fun. And school starts next week. This is the last of summer vacation; we need to make the most of it."

"Okay," Kriti said. "I guess it might be fun."

70

"DJ and I need to go home and change," said Taylor.

"And we need to get some things," added Eliza.

DJ wasn't even sure she wanted to go on this beach trip, plus she didn't like anyone, especially Taylor, speaking for her.

"I don't know if I'm going," she said in voice that sounded pretty grumpy, even to her ears.

"Are you still pouting because I beat you?" teased Taylor.

"No," said DJ. "I just don't know if I want to — "

"Come on, DJ," said Conner as he slipped his arm around her shoulders and gave her a warm squeeze. "Don't be a spoilsport."

She was about to say something mean, but that was when she noticed he was looking right into her eyes. And for a moment, she forgot everything else — everything but that clear, gorgeous shade of blue, deep and clear, just like the Atlantic Ocean.

"Okay," she said in a much more civilized, almost demure, tone. "But I do need to clean up."

"No problem," said Conner. "How about if we meet you guys at Carter House?"

"Sounds great," said Eliza cheerfully, digging around in her shiny white Prada bag. She pulled out her car keys that were attached to a large silver object. It looked more like jewelry than a key chain.

"And, with six of us, we'll definitely need to take both cars," said Harry. He dangled his keys in front of Conner's nose now. "You can drive my Jeep if I can ride with Eliza."

"Deal," said Conner eagerly reaching for the keys.

"Deal," said Eliza, nodding at Harry.

"Give us an hour or so," commanded Taylor, as if she alone were calling the shots. "DJ and I both need to clean up."

"How about noon?" suggested Eliza after checking her watch.

"See ya then," called Harry as he and Conner headed back toward his Jeep.

"This is going to be fun," said Eliza as they walked across the tennis court toward her Porsche.

"Oh, yeah," said Taylor. "Those guys are both really cute."

Eliza frowned slightly. "Maybe we should've asked them to invite some more guy friends to come along. I mean this is kind of lopsided — two guys and four girls."

"It's not as if we need to pair off," said Kriti a little indignantly. "That's certainly not why I'm going."

"Well, what about you, Taylor?" asked Eliza as she paused by her car. "Will you mind?"

"Mind what?" said Taylor quickly.

Eliza nodded toward DJ now. "Well, I sort of assume that Conner and DJ are a couple and that leaves you and Kriti both without—"

"You assume wrong," said Taylor as she set her bag and tennis racket into the front seat and then opened the door, pulled back the seat, and waited for Kriti to climb into the back. Then she got into the front passenger seat, the same spot she'd occupied on the way over. "DJ made it perfectly clear to me last night that she and Conner are only friends. Right, DJ?"

DJ and Kriti were both seated in the back now. And, although what Taylor was saying was true in essence, DJ felt it was wrong and unfair, not to mention manipulative. Still, she wasn't sure how to straighten this thing out.

"*Right*, DJ?" Taylor turned around in the front seat to scowl at DJ now. "You did say that you and Conner were simply friends, didn't you? It's not like I'm making this stuff up, am I?"

"I said we were friends," admitted DJ. "But that doesn't

mean it couldn't change. I mean, it's not like I can predict the future, but I do feel there's something special between us."

"Well, that's not how you sounded to me last night," said Taylor. "You were all like 'we're just friends, and that's all.'" She turned back around in the seat, speaking more to Eliza now. "If you ask me, that girl is flaky. She says one thing and then turns around and says something totally different."

"I am not flaky," said DJ. "I was just trying to be honest. Conner and I aren't officially a couple, but—"

"But it's a possibility," offered Eliza in a kind voice. "Don't pick on DJ, Taylor. I understand what she's saying. Maybe she thinks something is developing."

"Maybe she's wrong," said Taylor.

DJ gripped the handle of her tennis racket more tightly. It was all she could do not to raise it up and pop big-mouth Taylor over the head with it. Also, she was tempted to boy-cott this stupid beach party altogether—and she would have gladly—except for the disgusting thought of Taylor hotly pur-suing poor Conner in her absence.

DJ could just imagine Taylor grabbing Conner's hand as they were walking on the beach. She'd probably be wearing a skimpy bikini that showed off everything, including what DJ felt certain were silicone breast implants, as she tackled the poor guy down to the sand and then rolled in the surf, forc-ing him to make out with her. That image alone would ensure that DJ went along with this little field trip. Not only that, but today might need to be the day that she made her big play for Conner. Certainly, she wasn't really prepared for this. She had hoped their relationship, a really good friendship, might develop more slowly and steadily.

Feeling discouraged and beaten, DJ looked down at herself. She was wearing a frumpy old pair of gray sweat shorts along with a worn and faded blue Gap T-shirt that was still damp with perspiration and stretched out and frayed around the neck. Even DJ realized this outfit was not the least bit attractive, even if it was comfortable. But she hadn't been thinking of fashion when she dressed this morning; she had only been thinking of beating the snot out of Taylor.

And she hadn't expected Conner and his friend to show up like that. She wondered how Taylor had this figured out. Because who dresses up like that to play sports? Why would you want to get a nice outfit all sweaty? Well, obviously, girls like Taylor would. Girls like Taylor—and maybe Eliza and Kriti too—probably never went anywhere, not even to the emergency room to have a limb sewn back on, without looking their absolute best. They would probably freshen up their makeup while riding in the ambulance.

"Because," she could just hear her grandmother saying, "you just never know who you'll run into."

Well, DJ knew one thing: if she was going to compete with Taylor—and that seemed to be the case—it was high time she cleaned up her act. Not that she expected Conner to be taken in by appearances. Just last night he had made it clear that he wasn't that kind of a guy. Even so, DJ had seen him looking at Taylor. She was certain that he noticed the cleavage rising above her low-cut, snug-fitting, pink and white tennis shirt. She was sure he noticed those long brown legs in the short, short tennis skirt. Guys couldn't help but notice that kind of thing. They were guys, after all.

Still, DJ didn't have a clue as to what she was going to do or what she was going to wear to get Conner to look at her that way. Then, just as Eliza turned into the driveway, DJ remembered something. She remembered how, only last night, her grandmother had solicited assistance from these three girls, hinting that they might share some of their good style sense with her poor misguided and fashion-challenged granddaughter. She had practically begged these girls to help DJ improve her appearance.

As they walked into the house, DJ knew for a fact she would not be going to Taylor for help. That would be like asking the enemy if you could borrow a gun. No, she decided, she would go to Eliza. Privately. No way did she want Taylor to know what she was up to. She felt certain that Taylor would sabotage any attempt DJ made to compete with her.

"Hey, DJ," said Eliza as they paused at the foot of the steps. "Do you think it would be okay if we took something from here to eat at the beach? Or, maybe we should just pick something up on the way."

"We can probably find something here," said DJ, thinking this was her chance. "Want to go see what's available?"

"What are you doing?" asked Clara as DJ and Eliza stepped into her territory. DJ quickly told Clara their plans, which got Clara off the hook for having to serve and clean up lunch. Clara's eyes lit up. "Help yourselves," she said, pointing out what was on- and off-limits. She even got them an ice chest. "Do you girls think you'll be home in time for dinner?"

DJ glanced at Eliza.

"Maybe not," said Eliza. "Is that okay?"

"It's okay with me," said Clara happily. "Would you like me to inform Mrs. Carter? She went to town for a hair appointment."

"Yes," said DJ eagerly. "That'd be great."

"And there's some soda in the pantry," said Clara in a lowered voice, as if she expected to get into trouble. "Mrs. Carter wasn't too pleased that I bought it, but you could take it with you."

"Cool," said DJ.

"You girls run along," said Clara. "I'll get it all packed for you."

"Thanks so much," said Eliza. Then as she and DJ were going up the stairs, Eliza said, "Clara is really nice."

DJ laughed. "Yeah, she's nice because we're getting out of her hair and now she has the day off."

"Oh, I get it."

"Uh, Eliza," said DJ at the top of the stairs. "Can I ask a favor?"

"Of course."

So DJ quickly explained that she was starting to feel a little out of place. "I mean it's obvious that I have never taken fashion seriously. And the more Grandmother bugs me about it, the more I resist. Seriously, that woman makes me want to pull out my hair and scream. But now I'm wondering if I really do need some, uh, help."

Eliza laughed. "Duh, you need some help. I'm surprised your grandmother hasn't taken you in for a complete psychological evaluation by now, because I know she thinks you're totally crazy."

"The feeling's mutual."

"Okay, maybe Mrs. Carter takes fashion a little too seriously, but good grief, DJ, you could volunteer to be a permanent placeholder in the *fashion don't* section of *Style* magazine."

"That bad?" DJ sighed. "Is it hopeless?"

"Where there is life, there is hope. But we better get started ASAP." Right there in the hallway, Eliza looked carefully at DJ, scrutinizing every square inch of her. "Well, you have a lot going for you. You are naturally good-looking. The problem is you don't do anything with it."

"Because I don't know what to do."

76

Eliza nodded. Then she glanced toward the door to her room. "Kriti will probably get upset if I drag you in there. It's already too crowded. It'll help when we get some of our things moved downstairs. Inez is supposed to get on it today. In the meantime, let's go to your room."

As DJ led Eliza to her room, she had some serious doubts. What was she getting herself into? And was it a compromise of her values? What about what she'd told Conner last night? What about his concern over high-maintenance girls?

But her doubts were overshadowed by the image of Conner gazing at Taylor at the tennis court earlier, smiling at her with guy-like approval. She had definitely gotten his attention in a way that DJ never had. At least not yet.

8

mixed bags

"Stand right there," commanded Eliza as she practically shoved DJ in front of the full-length mirror on her closet door. DJ frowned at her own image. Talk about slumming. Next to Eliza she really did look like a *fashion don't*. Eliza's long hair was blonde and shiny. Her makeup was perfect. And her pale blue capri pants and white cropped top looked fresh and stylish, setting off her tan, which DJ suspected came from a bottle since she'd heard Eliza warning them all to use sunscreen this morning. Even Eliza's sandals and pink-polished toenails were perfect. Picture perfect.

"Let's start with the hat," said Eliza, snatching off DJ's Dodgers cap to reveal her mousy brown roots and hair that was in need of a good long shampoo. Eliza made a face as she tossed the cap to the floor. "DJ," she said in a scolding tone. "What is up with that hair?"

"I know ... it's dirty."

"Dishwater blonde and dirty."

DJ didn't say anything. She just looked down at her scuffed up blue and white Nikes—a leftover pair from JV volleyball, back before her mom died.

"And your clothes. Do you even *look* in the mirror?" She forced DJ's chin up with her hand. "Can you *see* yourself?"

DJ looked at herself now. She saw a flush-faced girl in dowdy clothes and greasy hair the color of—what had Eliza called it? Dishwater? Ugh, that did sound terrible.

"I'm a mess," she admitted.

"They say acceptance is the first step to recovery." Eliza shook her head in a dismal way. "But I have feeling you're going to need the whole twelve-step program."

"What's that?"

"A joke. It's a joke." Eliza leaned forward now and peered closely at DJ's skin. "What do you use to wash your face?"

"Soap?"

"What kind of soap?"

"The kind that's in the shower."

Eliza's brows shot up. "You use shower soap *on your face?*"

"Soap is soap, isn't it?"

But Eliza's expression suggested otherwise. In fact, if DJ hadn't known better, she might've assumed that Eliza thought she'd been washing her face with laundry detergent or maybe Lysol.

"Soap *is* soap, DJ," she said in a tightly controlled voice. "But soap is *not* for the face." She pointed to DJ's nose. "Can you see those blackheads?"

DJ felt alarmed. "You mean like pimples?" She leaned closer to peer at her nose and did notice there were tiny black spots on it. Maybe she'd thought those were freckles. She'd always thought it would be cool to have freckles.

"That's where pimples begin, DJ. And you need to cleanse them properly and not with some harsh soap." She let out a long sigh. "Where do I begin?" Then she looked at her watch again. "We don't quite have an hour."

"Maybe this is a mistake," said DJ. "I'm sorry I—"

"No, this is *not* a mistake. Trust me, DJ, this is not a mistake. It's just that it's a challenge. A really big challenge." She pushed DJ's shoulders back. "Stand up straight, please. Posture is as important as exfoliating."

"Exfo-what-ing?"

"Never mind." Eliza stood right next to DJ now, as if comparing their images in the mirror, which DJ felt was not only unkind, but unfair.

"What are you doing?"

"Trying to figure out if we're the same size. It looks close. What size are you anyway?"

"For what?"

"Everything. What size do you wear?"

"Well, for tops, I'm like a medium."

"A medium? I mean what *number* size."

"I don't know."

"Well, you don't look like a medium, that's for sure. But then everything I've seen you in is too baggy anyway. You probably are wearing medium, but you should be wearing small."

"I don't like things being too tight."

"How about your pants? You must know what size jeans you wear. I'm guessing a four ... maybe a six."

"More like six."

"Don't tell your grandmother, but I am too. And it looks like we're about the same height. Are you about five foot nine?

"Five ten." DJ stood straighter.

"Well, you never wear heels. It's hard to tell."

DJ thought that made no sense. Wasn't it harder to tell how tall people were who wore heels?

"Speaking of heels, what size shoe do you wear?"

81

"Nines."

"Hey, me too."

"Great," said DJ in a voice totally lacking in enthusiasm. She felt more pathetic than ever just now. It really was hopeless. Standing next to Eliza, all she could see were her flaws. She leaned over to stare at her nose again. She expected to see a zit appear at any moment.

"Okay, here's the plan," said Eliza quickly. "You get a quick shower and shampoo your hair really well, and I'll be right back."

"What should I use to wash my face?" asked DJ, feeling like she was about six years old now.

"Nothing for now. Just water. And shave your legs too. But hurry. We don't have much time."

So, still feeling utterly hopeless, DJ stripped off her sweaty clothes, threw them into the hamper, and leaped into the shower. She'd just gotten out and was towel drying her hair when Eliza popped in carrying an oversized plaid bag that appeared to be filled with all sorts of beauty products.

"Looks like you could be an Avon lady," teased DJ.

"Sit down there," commanded Eliza, pointing to a bench by the bathtub.

She'd changed into a pretty sky blue top and a pair of khaki shorts, complete with an attractive woven belt that matched her sandals. Perfect for a hot day on the beach—and just plain perfect.

DJ adjusted the towel that she'd wrapped around her like a sari and was barely seated on the bench before Eliza began messing with her hair.

"What are you doing?" asked DJ.

"Just putting some highlights on it. It's a product I keep handy for those times when I can't get to the salon. Just a little pick-me-up, until I can get professional help. I discovered it when my mom and I were touring Europe about a year ago. It works really great."

"Are you sure you know what you're doing?"

"Don't worry."

"How long does this stuff take?"

"Just fifteen minutes."

DJ's eyes began to water. Whatever Eliza was putting on her hair smelled like a combination of rotten eggs and formaldehyde — like something from chemistry class.

"What if my hair falls out?"

Eliza laughed. "It won't fall out."

DJ wasn't so sure. But she decided it might be safer to keep her mouth shut while Eliza was doing this. She didn't want to distract her. Before long, Eliza was done putting the stuff on her hair and she covered the top of her head with a piece of plastic. "Now your face," said Eliza, handing her a white tube of something. "This is an exfoliating cleanser. Just gently rub it into your face. But not around your eyes. Okay?"

"Is it dangerous?"

"No, silly. But avoid the eye area or you'll get puffy."

After that, Eliza handed her a warm, damp washcloth. "Now gently remove the cleanser with this, using small circular motions." DJ followed her instructions and then Eliza opened another small jar of something. "This is moisturizer with sunscreen. Just put a little on, here and here and here." She dotted it around on DJ's face. "And now gently rub it in."

"Hey, that feels pretty good," said DJ as she ran her fingertips over a cheek. "Smooth."

"Uh-huh," said Eliza as she handed her another tube of something. "Now, this is a bronzed moisturizer which also has sunscreen, and it's actually somewhat waterproof."

"What do I do with that?"

"Just rub it on the tops of your arms and on your legs and your chest. It's a way to get some color without endangering your skin." Then Eliza helped her, showing how much to use and how to blend it to look natural. "It'll come off if you go swimming."

DJ considered this. She wasn't sure that she wanted to don a swimsuit in front of Conner just yet. Besides that her only swimsuit was an old swim-team suit and she didn't really feel like wearing that in front of anyone. "I doubt that I'll go swimming," she told Eliza as she finished with the bronzer.

"Yeah, me too." Eliza pointed to her feet. "Now stick a footsie up on the edge of the tub."

"Why?"

"I want to check out those feet."

"My feet?"

"Yes!"

So DJ stuck a foot up on the edge of the tub, waiting for Eliza to tell her the next piece of bad news. Other than cutting her toenails occasionally, DJ rarely even looked at her feet.

"Well, there's nothing that a good pedicure won't fix. But we don't have time for that today. Still, rub some of this foot cream in and make sure you get each toe really saturated. Then just dab on a little bit of this clear polish for some sparkle."

Just as DJ finished her feet, Eliza noticed the time. She jumped up and said it was time to rinse off DJ's hair. "Stick your head in the tub," she commanded. Then she helped to rinse off whatever it was before she applied some conditioner that actually smelled pretty good. "We've got fifteen minutes," said Eliza as DJ towel dried her hair for the second time. "Come over to the mirror and let's do makeup."

"I don't think I'm much of a makeup girl," said DJ reluctantly. "I tried it a couple of times, but it looked pretty clownish on me."

"That's because you didn't do it right."

So Eliza helped her and when she was done, it wasn't too bad, although DJ thought she still looked a little silly.

"Now for wardrobe," said Eliza.

"That might be a challenge," said DJ as they went out of the bathroom. "My closet is pretty sparse and I—" DJ stopped in the doorway. There, on her bed, was a bunch of clothes that were not hers. "What?"

"These are just some things that I'm not that attached to. Plus, as you know, we're short on closet space. Why don't you give them a try?"

"But they're yours, Eliza, I can't—"

"Really, I have way too many clothes. I know this for a fact. You're doing me a favor. Okay?" She shoved some things at her. "Here, try these on and dry your hair. I want to go freshen up a little too."

For the next few minutes, DJ tried on several of the pieces that Eliza had donated. At first, it seemed a little strange wearing someone else's clothes. But they actually fit fairly well and looked pretty good too. Although DJ couldn't help but notice that the labels were not what she was used to, and she had a feeling they were expensive. She finally settled on a pair of pale denim shorts and a peasant-style sleeveless top. Not flashy, but comfortable and nice. She slipped on a pair of sand-colored platform sandals that looked like they were made out of twine and tied around her ankles. Not bad.

Then she went to the bathroom to dry her hair. At first she hadn't noticed much difference after Eliza's highlighting treatment, but once her hair was dry, she could see that it looked lighter and brighter and better. She studied her reflection with surprised interest, and she had to admit that it really was an improvement. Certainly, she wasn't as stunningly beautiful as Taylor, and she wasn't as picture-perfect pretty as Eliza or as exotic as Kriti, but she wasn't half bad either. In fact, she looked almost pretty.

She just hoped she looked pretty enough to turn Conner's head today. For some reason that meant more than anything to her just now. She hoped that it wasn't simply because of Taylor's interest in him. Or because DJ felt competitive and was trying to prove something. Because that seemed wrong. Still, she remembered how she'd felt spending time with Conner last night, how it almost seemed like a date, how he'd said sweet things to her, about her ... how it had seemed like maybe things really were changing between them. She hoped she wasn't wrong about that.

"Hey, DJ," yelled Eliza. "You ready?"

DJ emerged, stood in the center of the room with hands extended as if to show Eliza the results. Eliza smiled and gave a nod of approval. "Very nice."

"Thank you," said DJ, reaching for her old Fossil bag.

"Not that one," said Eliza quickly. She dug through the things splayed out on the bed until she found a sand-colored canvas bag trimmed in leather. In some ways, it didn't look that much different than DJ's Fossil bag, but she knew enough to know that it probably was.

"Hermès," said Eliza as she looped it over DJ's shoulder. "My mom picked it up in France and then decided she didn't like it. It's not really me, either, but I like it on you. You're more the natural type."

"The natural type?" DJ smiled. "I like that."

"You switch your stuff from your bag," said Eliza. "I need to get something."

Then, as DJ emerged from her room, she heard Taylor yelling up the stairway, "Come on you guys. Some of us are getting impatient."

"Coming," yelled DJ.

Just then Eliza came out holding up a sunglasses case. "Here," she said as she opened it up and slid a pair of shades onto DJ's nose. She stepped back to look. "Just what you need to top it off."

DJ attempted to peer at her image in the hallway mirror, but it was too dark to see much more than shadows.

"Trust me," said Eliza. "They're perfect."

DJ removed the shades, returned them to the case, and hugged Eliza. "Thank you," she said happily. "For everything."

Eliza chuckled. "I really should thank you, DJ."

"Why?"

"Well, if I tell you, you'll know just how shallow I actually am."

"Huh?"

"The truth is it's more fun to hang with a well-dressed girl than a street bum."

"Oh." Then DJ laughed. "Yeah, I guess I can understand that."

Harry was waiting with a picnic basket in the foyer downstairs. "Ready to go, ladies?"

"We need to get the ice chest too," said DJ.

"The cook already brought it out. I gave it to Conner to put in the Jeep." Harry grinned at Eliza. "I didn't think it would fit in your Porsche."

"Probably not," said Eliza.

"The others are outside," said Harry.

"Let's go," said Eliza.

As they went out, DJ was getting ready for what she hoped

would be Conner's reaction. If nothing else, he would at least do a double take. And then, as they were driving to the beach, he would probably mention something about her "new look." She wanted to be ready with a natural-sounding reaction. Some off-hand comment like, "I just took a shower and washed my hair. No biggie." Because no way did she want him to know this was her last-ditch desperate effort to keep his attention on her instead of Taylor.

But when they got outside, she realized that Conner was already sitting in the driver's seat of Harry's Jeep. And next to him, wearing the cattiest smile, was Taylor. In the backseat was Kriti.

Conner waved and smiled. "You want to ride with us, DJ?"

DJ looked uncertainly at Eliza.

"Or you can ride with us," said Eliza with a concerned frown, as if she knew.

"Come on," said Harry, tugging DJ toward the car. "I'd love to ride around Crescent Cove in a Porsche with a couple of beautiful babes."

DJ waved at Conner. "That's okay. You guys already have three in the car. I'll even things out and go with Harry and Eliza."

Taylor nodded with an expression that seemed to shout, "I win! I win!"

DJ stood straighter now, forcing a smile as she climbed into the back of Eliza's Porsche, next to the picnic basket. Then she opened the Hermès bag and retrieved the sunglasses case that Eliza had just given her. She slipped on the shades, hoping their oversized lenses might help to conceal her emotions, because at the moment, she felt like she could either burst into tears or go into a hysterical rage.

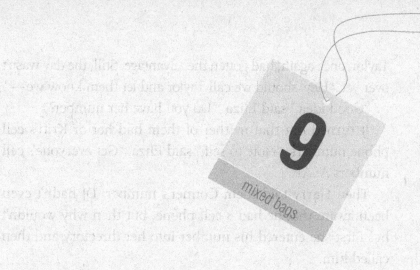

9

mixed bags

Eliza had only gone a few blocks when DJ noticed that the ride seemed a little bumpy. She stuck her head out the window and looked down to see that the Porsche's left rear tire looked odd.

"Hey, Houston, I think we've got a problem."

"What?"

"I think you might have a flat tire."

Eliza pulled over and sure enough, the tire was flat. Fortunately, Harry said, "No problem," rolled up his sleeves, and located the jack and spare tire.

"I could call Triple A," said Eliza.

"This'll be quicker," he said, putting the jack into place.

"Plus, it'll be educational," said DJ with interest. "I've never changed a tire before."

"Wanna help?" asked Harry.

"No," said Eliza quickly. "She doesn't." Then as Harry worked on the car, she quietly reminded DJ that they'd just gotten her cleaned up. "I don't want you to ruin my hard work."

"Right." But DJ was thinking it didn't really matter now.

Taylor, once again, had gotten the advantage. Still, the day wasn't over yet. "Hey, should we call Taylor and let them know we—"

"Good idea," said Eliza. "Do you have her number?"

It turned out that neither of them had her or Kriti's cell phone numbers. "Note to self," said Eliza. "Get everyone's cell numbers ASAP."

Then Harry told them Conner's number. DJ hadn't even been aware that he had a cell phone, but then why wouldn't he? First she entered his number into her directory and then called him.

"Hey," he said, his low voice catching her off guard.

"This is DJ," she began quickly, suddenly nervous to be talking to him on the phone. "We got a flat tire."

"Bummer. Want us to come back and help?"

"No, Harry's got it under control. We just wanted to let you know that we'd be running a little behind."

"That's okay. We're not going anywhere at the moment anyway."

"Why?"

"We stopped at the store."

"The store?"

"Yeah, just the Shop 'n' Go. Taylor needed to pick up something. Kriti and I are out in the parking lot waiting for her."

"Oh, well, guess we'll see ya at the beach then."

"Right." There was a pause and DJ wasn't even sure if he was still on or not. "You know, DJ, I thought you were going to ride with me and Kriti in the Jeep, and then Taylor hopped in the front, and I didn't know what to—"

"It's okay," said DJ in a falsely cheerful voice. "Eliza and I weren't moving too fast."

"Well, here comes Taylor now. See ya down there."

DJ felt a tiny bit better when she hung up, knowing that

Conner felt a little bit bad for how it had gone back at the house. That was something. After about fifteen more minutes, Harry had the tires switched and they were back on the road again.

"Don't forget to get that flat tire fixed," he warned Eliza.

"Oh, yeah," she said. "But how do I do that?"

He chuckled and then explained to her the concept of tire stores.

"I know I probably sound dumb," she admitted. "But I'm used to having other people take care of that kind of thing."

"I'm happy to help you," he offered.

She turned and smiled brightly at him. "Thanks, Harry. That's good to know."

Soon they were driving down a private road that seemed to lead to the beach. But the road was sandy and rutted and DJ was worried that Eliza's car might get stuck.

"I hope it doesn't get much worse than this," said Eliza as they bumped along. "My car's not exactly an off-road vehicle, you know."

"We're almost there," Harry assured her. "Just take it easy, and you'll be fine."

"Just don't get another flat tire," called DJ from the back. "Or else we'll be stuck."

But soon the road opened out into what looked like a small, sandy parking lot, where several other vehicles were already parked.

"Whose cars?" asked Eliza.

"Just locals," said Harry, pointing over to where his Jeep was parked. "You have to know the right people to use this road and park down here."

"And you do?" asked DJ.

"Yeah, my family has a beach house right over there."

91

He pointed down the beach as he got the picnic basket out of the backseat.

"Cool," Eliza said as she got a blanket out of her trunk.

"Yeah, I get to use it for parties sometimes, but this weekend my parents loaned it out to some friends."

"Should I put the top up?" Eliza asked Harry.

"Nah. Just don't leave any valuables in your car. It's pretty safe here, but you never know. I figure you're better off to just leave the top down. A friend had his convertible broken into, and the cost of replacing the slashed top was a lot more than the CDs that got stolen."

They headed down a sandy path bordered by tall beach grass, and soon they were out on a nice stretch of beach. It looked like about twenty or thirty other kids were already there. Not exactly a party, because they were sort of spread out, but as Harry walked past a small group of sunbathers, some of the girls called out to him. He called back, "Hey," and DJ noticed that a couple of the girls in that group were familiar. Painfully familiar. But she didn't actually look at them, and she had a feeling they didn't recognize her. Even if they did, they probably wouldn't remember her anyway.

"Who were they?" asked Eliza, once they were out of earshot.

"Girls from school," said Harry.

"I recognized a couple of them," said DJ. "Madison and Tina." As soon as she said those two names, she was left with a bad taste in her mouth.

"Sounds like you don't like them much," said Eliza.

"More like they don't like me much."

"Those two can be mean," said Harry. "I don't get that though. Why do girls get so mean?" Before anyone could answer, he pointed to where Conner and Kriti were just setting up some beach chairs next to the big white ice chest that Taylor was sitting on.

"Nice of you guys to set up camp for us," said DJ as they joined them.

"I didn't realize I was going to be used as a pack mule," said Taylor, pretending to wipe sweat from her forehead.

"Yeah, right," said Kriti, who actually was sweating. "I think Conner and I brought up most of the stuff."

"I helped carry the cooler," said Taylor as she unsnapped her western-style shirt to reveal a very small bikini top that looked like it had been constructed from a crocheted doily, the kind DJ's great-aunt Margaret used to have on all her tables. DJ tried not to stare, but she was curious as to how Taylor managed to keep all those little holes in the right places. She also wondered how well that top would hold up in saltwater. Or maybe Taylor didn't plan to go swimming.

"Hey, matching purses," said Taylor when she spotted DJ's new bag.

"Except that yours is Hype," pointed out Kriti as she nudged the similar bag with the toe of her sandal, "My dad won't even copy Hype."

"It's just a beach bag," said Taylor defensively.

Now Kriti was eying DJ's bag closely. "And DJ's bag just happens to be Hermès."

"No way," said Taylor, staring at the bag too.

"Way," said Kriti. "And it's the real thing too."

Taylor suddenly looked at DJ more carefully. "Hey, what's up with you anyway, DJ? Did you have a makeover?"

"Just cleaned up," said DJ as she tossed her bag down on one of the blankets and then opened the cooler to remove a soda.

"You clean up good," said Conner, winking at her.

"Want a soda?" she asked him while the cooler was still open.

"Or maybe Conner wants something a little more exciting," said Taylor as she opened a large paper grocery bag and pulled out a six-pack of brown bottles. "Something with a little more zing."

"Is that beer?" asked Conner.

"It is," said Taylor with a sly grin. "India Pale Ale, actually."

"Your stop at the store was to buy beer?" he asked with a frown.

Then she pulled out another six-pack. "Beer and wine coolers. I thought the ladies might prefer something a little—"

"How did you buy those?" demanded Kriti.

"With *money*."

"No, I mean how did you buy booze when you're underage?" persisted Kriti. The others waited for Taylor's answer.

"I have ID."

"You mean *fake* ID." Kriti folded her arms across her chest and scowled. "I cannot believe you did that, Taylor. While Conner and I were waiting, you were in there buying wine and beer and then you put it into the car. We could all get into serious trouble and—"

"Don't freak," said Harry in a soothing voice. "Lots of kids bring beer down to the beach. It's not that big of a deal, Kriti. I've never seen anyone getting busted down here."

"And then they drive?" demanded Kriti. "Under the influence?"

"I'm not driving," said Taylor as she opened a wine cooler and took a swig and then sat down on a beach chair. "Anyone else?"

"I'm not driving," said Harry as he reached for a beer.

DJ wasn't sure what to do now. She wasn't into drinking. But she didn't want to look like a spoiler either. She glanced at Conner who seemed to be a little unsettled too. Then she looked at Eliza, who seemed perfectly fine.

"A little bit of wine never hurt anyone," said Eliza as she reached for a wine cooler. Then she looked at the label more carefully. "Not that this is a very good wine. Good grief, Taylor, I thought you had better taste than this."

"Hey, it was a convenience store, not a wine shop."

"Well, at least it's chilled," said Eliza as she opened it and sniffed. "Oh, my, what a delightful bouquet. I smell a trace of imitation berry extract with undertones of cheap wine. Lovely."

"No one's making you drink it," said Taylor.

"This is good," said Harry. "I compliment your taste in beers, Taylor."

"Thank you," said Taylor happily. "It's nice to see we have a connoisseur in our midst."

"Why don't you try one too, Conner," suggested Harry.

Conner shrugged. "I'm not into beer."

"Maybe that's because you haven't tasted good beer," said Harry. He reached for a second one and handed it to Conner. "Just try it, man. You might be surprised."

Conner looked even more conflicted now.

"Come on, Conner," urged Taylor. "Be a big boy and try it. If you don't like it, you don't have to drink it." She laughed. "Besides, you don't want to make Harry, Eliza, and I drink all twelve bottles by ourselves. Let's see ... that would be like four bottles apiece. And, don't forget, Eliza is driving, so we'll have to cut her off sooner than that."

Kriti looked steaming mad now. She started to say something but then just turned and walked away. They all watched as she

95

stomped off down the beach. DJ considered going after her, but didn't like the idea of leaving this particular foursome alone. Or more specifically, she didn't like the idea of leaving Taylor with Conner.

"She'll cool off," said Taylor. "She just needs to grow up a little."

"She's been very protected," said Eliza as she leaned back in the beach chair. "Ahh ... this feels good."

"Why don't you guys sit down?" said Harry, pointing to Conner and DJ. "You're making the rest of us feel uncomfortable."

"And why don't you try a wine cooler, DJ," said Taylor. "Or are you like Kriti—a teetotaler too?"

"I already have a soda," DJ pointed out as she sat down on the blanket and took a sip. She didn't want to stare at Conner, but she was curious to see if he was going to let them pressure him into drinking a beer. Then he sat down beside her, opened the bottle, and took a cautious sip.

"So, Conner," said Taylor, "how is it?"

Conner wrinkled his nose a little. "Kind of bitter."

"It's beer, man," said Harry. "It's not supposed to be sweet. Take another sip. It's an acquired taste, you know."

DJ watched as Conner took another sip and his face grew thoughtful as if he were still trying to figure out whether or not he liked it.

"Did you know that the drinking age in Connecticut *used* to be eighteen?" said Harry.

"Really?" said Taylor with interest. "Why did they raise it?"

"According to my parents, the state lowered it in the seventies. They figured that if eighteen-year-olds could be drafted for Vietnam, they should be able to drink too. And they changed the law."

"So when did they change it back?" asked Eliza.

"In the eighties. Thanks to Mother's Against Drunk Driving."

"Those crazy MADD women," said Taylor. "I think Kriti must be a secret member."

They all laughed. Then Taylor pointed at Conner who was still holding a beer. "So? What do you think of the beer now?"

"Tastes like something that an old pair of my dirty sweat socks has been soaking in for a week or two." Then he put the lid back on, shoved it into the sand, and turned to DJ who was leaning against the cooler. "Wanna get me a Coke outta there, DJ?"

She grinned at him and reached for a soda. Then he popped it open, holding up the can like he wanted to toast her, and she grinned as they clicked cans together.

"Here's to sobriety," he said loudly.

"And to designated drivers," she added.

"Fine," said Taylor. "That leaves more for the three of us." But the tone of her voice suggested that she was not at all pleased. Still, DJ couldn't help but smile to herself as she sipped her Coke. It felt as if she might've just won round three. Or was it round four? And then she wondered how many rounds there would be before it was over. Because Taylor seemed like the kind of girl who usually got what she wanted. And she did not seem like the kind of girl who gave up easily.

"Hey, there's food in the cooler if anyone's hungry," said DJ when she noticed that Taylor and Harry were both more than half-way through their second alcoholic beverage now. "You big drinkers might want to put something solid in your tummies to offset that booze."

"Thanks, *Mom*," sniped Taylor, taking a long swig as if to prove she was totally unconcerned.

Just the same, DJ went ahead and got some of the food items out, arranging them on the blanket so that everyone could easily help themselves. The guys seemed to appreciate this, although Eliza and Taylor seemed uninterested in eating as they sipped their wine coolers and acted silly. Or maybe they were more obsessed with weight than DJ realized. Whatever. DJ wasn't going to force them to eat. After all, what difference did it make to her? They were her grandmother's responsibility, not hers.

Still, she felt a little worried. And it bugged her to feel like this. She didn't want to get stuck playing the "mom" role with the Carter House girls. Like how fair was that? Even so, she was also thinking about Kriti. She'd been gone nearly an hour by now, and DJ had no idea where she was or if she was okay. She wondered if someone should go out looking for her.

DJ was about to mention her concern to the others, but suddenly realized that this would only risk Taylor making another "mom" joke at DJ's expense. Maybe she could talk Conner into looking for Kriti. Better yet, maybe she and Conner could both go to search for their missing friend. That would also be a good escape from Taylor and her endless jabs. DJ suspected Taylor's nastiness might grow even worse under the influence of alcohol. DJ remembered hearing that people's true personalities came out when they were wasted. She hated to imagine how mean someone like Taylor might get, and DJ definitely did not want to be in that girl's line of fire.

DJ was mentally preparing a strategy for getting Conner and her away from the others, as she removed a large bowl of pasta salad from the cooler (more of those forbidden carbs that her grandmother had been warning Clara to avoid). But just as she stood, she observed Taylor bent over and fishing around in DJ's new Hermès bag. What was up with that?

"Hey, Taylor," said DJ trying not to sound as irate as she felt for this invasion of privacy, "what're you doing?"

"Getting my cigarettes, if you don't mind," snapped Taylor. "I know you *think* you're my mom, but hopefully you're not getting on my case for smoking now. There seems to be plenty of air to go around out here."

"You've got the *wrong* bag," said DJ as she retrieved some plates and silverware from the picnic basket, setting them out by the salad.

"That's right." Eliza nodded, pointing to the purse. "That's DJ's bag, Taylor. You must have made a Freudian slip. You just *wished* the Hermès was yours." Eliza threw back her head and laughed.

DJ had to laugh too. This joke was totally on Taylor. Then, just as DJ was setting a veggie platter on the blanket, she heard Taylor starting to snicker loudly. DJ glanced over to see what was so amusing, and Taylor still had her hands inside DJ's Hermès bag.

"Taylor!" DJ was aggravated now. "Give it up, will you? I guarantee that you will not find any cigarettes in *my* bag. Okay?"

But Taylor just smiled—she smiled in a way that DJ, in hindsight, would describe as *purely evil.* "Oh, but I did find something else, DJ—something even more interesting—especially from a goody-goody girl like you." Then Taylor removed something small from the Hermès bag and held it up. From where she was standing, DJ couldn't see what was in Taylor's hand, but the others were starting to laugh now. Not loudly, but more of an embarrassed kind of laugh—sort of like an uncomfortable titter.

"Huh?" DJ went closer now, peering at whatever Taylor was holding up and acting so pleased about. The shiny items in her hands looked like tiny foil packets, like maybe they were samples of gum or candy or something. "What are those?" asked DJ.

"Condoms, of course!" exploded Taylor as she shook the shiny objects in front of DJ's face. "You really do come prepared for everything, don't you, DJ?" She looked toward the boys now. "My question is who did you plan to use these with?"

DJ felt her cheeks grow instantly hot as she stared at those totally foreign objects. "Those are *not mine!*" she hissed at Taylor.

"No, no, of course, they're not." Taylor was using her low seductive voice now. "I'm sure that's why they were in the pocket of your Hermès bag, because they are most definitely *not yours*."

"They're *not!*" DJ reached over and snatched her bag away from Taylor.

"Yeah, right." Taylor was laughing even harder now. "You are full of surprises, DJ. Just when I thought you were such a—"

"I swear, they're not mine," insisted DJ. "You probably planted them there, Taylor. Just to embarrass me. I'm sure you've got plenty of those things in your purse." She reached for Taylor's bag now, ready to prove her point and clear her name in front of Conner and the others.

"Go ahead and look all you want," said Taylor in a totally unconcerned voice. "And while you're at it, could you toss me my cigarettes? That's all I was looking for anyway. Sorry to expose your little secrets."

DJ knew it would be futile to look in Taylor's bag. Taylor was not that careless. If this was a setup, she'd probably made sure to have nothing incriminating in her bag. So DJ tossed the bag at Taylor, throwing it so hard that a strap flew up and hit Taylor in the chin.

"Ouch!" shouted Taylor with narrowed eyes. "You don't need to get violent."

DJ looked helplessly at Eliza now. "Tell Taylor that those things weren't mine," she commanded her.

"Why should I tell her that?" Eliza's brow creased with a slightly wounded expression.

"Because they must've been yours. You're the one who gave me that bag in the first place, Eliza. So, obviously, they must be yours, *right?*" DJ felt more desperate than ever.

Eliza just shook her head. "I hardly think so, DJ. Good grief, talk about looking a gift horse in the mouth. And to think I thought we were friends."

102

"Well, they must be your mom's then, Eliza. You said she bought this bag in France originally. Maybe she put them in the bag and—"

"You should watch what you insinuate about other people's mothers," warned Eliza. "A person might get offended."

DJ knew that her face was flaming red now. She couldn't remember ever feeling this totally degraded before. If this morning's tennis match had seemed bad, this was worse. Way, way worse. She so didn't want Conner to see her like this. And, more than that, she didn't want to look at him either. She couldn't imagine looking into his eyes now. All she wanted was to get away—far, far away. So, with the detestable Hermès bag still in her hands, she turned her back to the group, who had now grown quiet and, feeling like she was doing a bad Kriti imitation, she headed down the beach in the same direction that Kriti had stomped off. As she hurried away, she had no doubts that her "friends" would soon be making fun of her behind her back too.

After a few minutes, DJ was torn between the desire to get even and simply to get away. She even considered calling her dad on her cell phone, begging him to take her back, promising him that she'd do whatever it took. Maybe Jan and the twins weren't so horrible after all. They might've been demanding, but they had never humiliated her before. At least not intentionally. Cleaning house, doing laundry, even changing smelly diapers—what were those chores compared to feeling this miserable?

She wasn't sure how long or how far she had walked, but she did realize that she'd reached a part of the beach that seemed fairly uninhabited. On one hand, it was a relief to be away from the others, but on the other hand, it was a little unnerving too. What if she ran into some kind of pervert?

She was just about to turn back when she saw someone quite a way down the beach. At first she thought it was a child, but then she realized it was Kriti, slowly walking toward her. For no rational reason, DJ's heart went out to Kriti just then. She felt terrible for not standing up for Kriti earlier. Maybe it was simply the sort of empathy that is born from a similar experience. But DJ began to walk faster, waving and calling out Kriti's name.

"What are you doing?" asked Kriti when they finally met.

"Running away from home," said DJ.

"Huh?"

"Taylor just managed to totally humiliate me."

"How?"

So DJ told her the whole skanky, sordid story. Ironically, it didn't seem quite as bad when she said it all out loud. In fact, she almost expected Kriti to laugh. But she didn't.

"Taylor is wicked mean," said Kriti.

DJ nodded. "I'll say."

"I was thinking about calling my parents and asking to come home," admitted Kriti.

"Me too."

"Really?" Kriti frowned. "But isn't the Carter House sort of like your home? I mean isn't Mrs. Carter your grandmother?"

"No and yes. She's my grandmother, but the Carter House doesn't really feel like home."

"Where is your home?"

DJ realized that Kriti didn't really know much about her, so she told her the shortened version of her mother's death and how it hadn't worked out so great with her dad and his new wife and twin girls. "Still, I was just thinking I might be willing to go back and play nanny now. It would be better than being tortured by Taylor."

"I'm curious, DJ." Kriti frowned. "What does your grandmother think of these things? Underage drinking ... smoking ... lying ... meanness ... and other forms of wayward behavior."

DJ tried not to cringe at the "wayward behavior" thing. Kriti sounded as if she were quoting her parents. "Well, as you know, my grandmother has rules."

"I know about the rules. I signed the contract, DJ."

"So you're asking if she enforces her rules."

"Exactly."

DJ shrugged. "The truth is, I don't know."

Kriti slowly nodded. "I thought as much."

"Does that worry you?"

Kriti seemed to consider this. "It does make me feel a little insecure, but I do know that all I need to do is call my parents and they will rescue me."

"Do you feel like you need to be rescued?"

"I wasn't sure," she confessed. "I was prepared to come back to the group and discover that everyone was inebriated. In that case, I would call my parents. I know they would not allow me to ride with a drunk driver."

"Do you drive?"

She shook her head. "No."

"Well, I do. And I don't plan to let Eliza drive home. And I suspect Conner will drive for Harry."

"Conner didn't imbibe?"

"No. He took a little sample of beer and didn't like it. He and I were only drinking soda."

Kriti almost smiled now. "That is a relief."

Now DJ put an arm around Kriti's shoulders. "I'm sorry, Kriti. I should've stood up for you. But I was falling for the old peer-pressure thing."

Now Kriti did smile. "Thank you, DJ. I appreciate that."

DJ sighed and looked up at the sky. Her best guess was that it was about three o'clock and probably too soon to talk everyone into going home. Besides that, it was an absolutely gorgeous day, not nearly as hot as yesterday. "So, what do we do now?"

Kriti shrugged. "I'm not sure that I want to go back yet."

"Me either." Then DJ remembered something. "Do you know how to play volleyball?"

Kriti brightened. "I was on the team in middle school."

"There was a game going on somewhere up there," DJ said as she pointed.

"I don't think they were playing when I walked by, but I noticed the net."

"Should we go see if they take walk-ons?"

Kriti grinned. "Sounds fun."

So they walked back up to where two teams were playing. One team, a little short-handed, only had three players—two guys and a girl. The other team had four, and three of them were fairly athletic-looking guys. Kriti and DJ just stood and watched for a couple of minutes, but it looked like the small team was getting soundly beaten.

"Need any more players?" called out DJ.

"Sure," said a dark-haired girl on the team of three. She had just missed a low shot and was brushing sand off her hands. "Maybe we won't have to work so hard."

A guy on the team of four yelled, "We get the tall chick."

"No way," said the dark-haired girl. "You guys are already creaming us."

"How about if you take both of us in a package deal?" suggested DJ. "It'll be uneven whichever way you cut it, and it looks like your team is already behind."

"Yeah," said one of the jocks on the team of four. "We're doing just fine the way we are. You losers can take both the chicks."

"Thanks a lot," yelled the dark-haired girl as she waved DJ and Kriti to her side of the net. "I'm Leah," she told them, quickly introducing everyone around.

They repositioned themselves and soon started playing again. And it wasn't long before DJ could tell that the team of four was regretting this small rearrangement. All the players seemed surprised at how well both DJ and Kriti played. In fact, DJ was surprised that, for a half-pint, Kriti was a real fireball. After a few minutes, the tables turned, and the underdog team made a comeback, winning the last two games out of three. To show their appreciation, Leah insisted that DJ and Kriti stay for a soda. "Are you from around here?" she asked.

DJ explained that they had both recently moved to Crescent Cove and would be attending high school there in town.

"That's cool," said Leah. "Except that we'll be rivals. We go to JFK High, and Crescent is one of the schools in our conference."

"One of our most competitive schools," said a guy named Luke.

"Usually, we're in the playoffs together," said Leah.

"Then maybe we'll see you at some games," said DJ.

"Volleyball?" asked the girl with a slight frown.

"Yeah," said DJ. "If I make the cut."

Leah laughed. "You'll make the cut."

"How about you, Kriti?" asked DJ.

Kriti sort of shrugged. "I'm pretty short."

"But you are totally quick," said Leah.

"You should try out," said DJ. "It'd be fun."

Kriti nodded. "I'll think about it."

"Hey, you girls coming?" called one of the guys. "We're picking new teams, and we want both DJ and Kriti in the lineup this time."

So they agreed to play some more. DJ felt only a teeny bit bad for having abandoned their so-called friends up the beach. She figured they wouldn't be missed much. But then, just as they were midway through their third game, and having a total blast, she noticed that standing among the growing group of spectators was Conner. And then, not long after that, he was joined by Taylor, Harry, and Eliza. DJ totally ignored them, playing hard and playing well. She felt a little bad when she spiked the ball straight into Kriti, but then Kriti made a noble effort to set it up. Still, DJ's team won. They all hugged and gave high fives, and DJ told the kids that she wished she was going to their high school.

"Really?" said Leah. "That's so sweet."

"Why don't you transfer?" said Luke.

DJ kind of laughed. "You know, if I thought that were even slightly possible, I think I would make an attempt."

"Then look into it," said Leah.

DJ nodded. "Looks like our friends are here. I guess we better go."

"Thanks for playing," called Leah. "And for leading our team to victory!"

DJ waved at Leah then braced herself as she and Kriti slowly went over to join the others. During the volleyball game, she had almost forgotten about her embarrassing episode with Taylor. Almost.

"Eew!" said Taylor as she literally turned up her nose at DJ. "Someone needs a shower."

They were packing up the picnic things now, and DJ had not spoken a word to Taylor. She was trying to ignore her. But that last comment was just too much. "Someone needs to learn manners," said DJ, standing up and facing Taylor now.

"I suppose you think *you* can teach me." Taylor looked at DJ as if she were a pile of stinking garbage. "And what is that brownish gunk all over your shirt? It looks like you've been rolling in something. No wonder you smell."

DJ looked down at her white peasant shirt, the shirt that had looked so fresh and pretty when they'd left the house. It now had brownish streaks here and there. She'd been so absorbed in the volleyball game that she hadn't noticed. Suddenly she remembered the bronzing lotion that Eliza had shared with her this morning. Obviously, it was not sweat proof. DJ locked eyes with Taylor, and for a brief insane moment she considered actually slapping her right across her pretty face. Instead, she just gave her a piece of her mind.

"You are the meanest, rudest girl I have ever met. No

wonder your mother couldn't wait to get rid of you." Then DJ turned away, stormed straight toward the ocean and walked right in. Fine, if she needed a shower, she might as well take a bath. The water was cold, but she just kept wading until the waves were at her waist. And then she began to swim. She was surprised at how quickly she adjusted to the stinging cold. It actually felt good, and it distracted her from what was back on the beach. And it felt good to swim too. She considered swimming and swimming and never turning back. But then she realized that someone, probably Kriti, would get worried and call the coast guard to pick her up. And that would be even more humiliation.

So she turned back. She was surprised at how far she'd gone. She couldn't even see the beach from out there. Still, she knew she was a good swimmer and there was nothing to be alarmed about. She could swim for hours if necessary. And so what if she worried her so-called friends (excluding Kriti who she felt might have the potential to be a real friend).

She was getting a little tired when she saw something splashing in the water ahead of her. And for one horrifying moment she considered the possibility of sharks. Then she realized it was a person.

"DJ!" yelled a guy's voice. "Are you okay?"

She peered at the wet head bobbing in the waves and finally realized it was Conner. She swam a little faster, and finally she was face-to-face with him. "I'm perfectly fine," she said, although her teeth were chattering now.

"We thought you'd drowned."

She rolled her eyes. "They probably just wished I'd drowned."

"Maybe Taylor did," admitted Conner.

"Well, good, I hope that it really upsets her when she sees

110

that I'm alive." They were swimming back now. "Why did you come out here, Conner?" she asked, noticing that his swimming stroke wasn't as strong as hers.

"I was worried."

"I'm a good swimmer," said DJ.

"Yeah, I can see that."

"Are you okay?" She frowned at him.

"Yeah, I'm fine."

"Because I've had lifesaving classes. I could rescue you if I had to."

He kind of laughed. "Good to know."

"But I might have to knock you over the head. I heard that if a victim gets freaked, and they're bigger than you, you have to knock them out to get them safely back."

He chuckled. "I don't think you'll have to knock me out, DJ."

"What if I want to?"

Now Conner really laughed. "Why?"

"Maybe I just have the need to punch someone today." She made a growling sound. "Taylor is driving me nuts. It's like she's determined to torture me. That whole thing about the bag . . . it took every ounce of self-control not to let her have it."

"She's just jealous."

"Jealous?" Now DJ laughed. But it was a sarcastic laugh. Still it slowed down her swimming. But it seemed that Conner was slowing down too.

"Taylor is jealous of you, DJ. Isn't it obvious?"

"No. She beat me in tennis. She humiliated me in front of everyone by switching our bags. She insults me and says I stink, and you think—"

"I think she wouldn't give you this grief if she wasn't jealous."

"Yeah, well, whatever." She continued swimming in silence now. It seemed unlikely that the stunningly beautiful Taylor—poor little rich girl, daughter of Eva Perez—would be jealous of someone like DJ. But, whatever.

Then she noticed that Conner had paused, he seemed to be just treading water, bobbing up and down in the waves.

"What's wrong?" she asked as she looked back at him. His face looked serious, and for a moment she thought he really was drowning. She moved back toward him. "Are you okay? Did you get a cramp? We're not that far from the shore."

Just then he reached out, grabbed one of her arms, and pulled her toward him. She briefly wondered if she might actually need to hit him over the head right now. Maybe this boy did need rescuing. But then he pulled her so close that her face was just inches from his. He was looking straight into her eyes with a very intense stare. "DJ!" he said in a firm voice.

"What?" she barely whispered.

"Taylor is jealous of you because she knows that I really like you."

"You do?" She noticed that his eyes were the exact same color as the ocean.

He nodded. "But I don't think you feel the same way."

"You don't?"

"No, you keep running away from me."

"I'm not running away. I'm getting pushed away."

He pulled her closer now, wrapping his arms around her as they both continued to tread water, rocking gently in the waves. "I'm not the one who's pushing you away."

"No . . ." It felt slightly difficult to breathe just now, but DJ didn't think it was because she was tired.

"So, how do you feel?"

She smiled now. "I like you."

Then he pulled her close, and the next thing she knew his lips were pressing into hers. And there was a warm sensation, a wonderful salty, warm sensation that started at her lips then rushed all the way through her to her toes. They kissed several times, and suddenly they were both breathless and struggling to stay above water.

"We better get back to shore," he said as he pulled her by one hand and began swimming again.

She nodded. And they both swam without speaking until their feet finally touched the sandy bottom. Then they stood and looked at each other. Conner was smiling in a pleased yet slightly surprised way. DJ figured her face probably looked very similar. Then he pulled her toward him for another kiss, and just as their lips touched a big wave came from behind and rolled them over. They both came up sputtering and laughing. Then, holding hands, they waded back to the beach.

They paused at the water's edge where Conner sweetly pushed the hair away from her face. "You might want to do something about your blouse," he said shyly, not even looking down.

That's when she noticed that the soggy white peasant blouse was now clinging to her like Saran wrap. Consequently, her bra and everything else seemed to be shining through. She fluffed out the fabric as best she could, hoping the sunshine would dry it quickly. At least the brown streaks were gone now.

"Ready to go back and face the frightening mob?" asked Conner as he took her hand again.

She nodded. "I am."

And so the two of them, hand in hand, marched back to where the others were all sitting on the sand, obviously waiting.

"So DJ didn't drown after all," said Taylor in what seemed a disappointed voice.

"I rescued her," said Conner.

DJ gave him a playful punch in the arm. "I didn't need rescuing."

"Actually, I thought she was going to have to rescue me," he admitted. "We even discussed the possibility of knocking me out so she could haul me back in to shore."

"You were doing just fine," she told him, smiling up into his face.

"Can we go now?" demanded Taylor. "It's almost seven o'clock and some of us have a life."

"And, as you can see, your designated drivers have arrived," said Conner. He held out his hand for Harry's keys.

Harry shook his head. "Oh, I'm okay now, buddy. I'll drive."

"We had an agreement," said Conner in a stern tone.

DJ reached out for Eliza's keys now. "I can drive for you too."

Eliza frowned as if unconvinced, but at least she handed over her keys. "Well, I think I'd be fine, but if you insist."

"She insists," said Kriti. "And if you don't let her drive, I'm not riding with you."

"Fine, fine," said Eliza in a tired voice. "Let's just get this show on the road. I'm tired, and I think I'm getting a sunburn." She patted her flushed face.

"Oh, that's just the alcohol," said Harry as he reluctantly handed the keys to Conner. "My old man always gets flushed like that when he's had too much."

Eliza groaned as she examined her face in the mirror in her compact. "Ugh, I look terrible."

"Who cares?" said DJ lightly.

Taylor laughed her mean laugh. "Obviously, *not you*."

Conner turned and looked at DJ with warm eyes. "I think DJ looks beautiful."

"Oh, man," said Taylor. "Get me outta here."

Harry was reaching for Eliza now. "Why don't you ride with me, gorgeous?"

She smiled at him. "Don't mind if I do."

"We'll let Conner play chauffeur while we occupy the backseat."

She giggled.

"I'll ride with you guys too," said Taylor quickly.

Now Conner frowned. "I have an idea. "Why don't the girls all ride together, and I'll drive Harry."

There was some argument because it seemed the group had been discussing the possibility of going to town together and taking in a movie. But Conner convinced everyone that he and DJ both needed to get home to change out of their wet clothes. "We can meet up again later." Then as they were about to get in their separate cars, Conner paused to bend down and kiss DJ right in front of everyone. It was only on the cheek, but it was nice. Very nice.

"Take care," he told her as he let go of her hand.

She felt her face getting warm as she nodded. "See ya."

The other girls were already in Eliza's car, and she could feel them watching. They were quiet as she started the engine, but as soon as she began to drive, Eliza turned and looked at her. "What's up with you and Conner?"

"What do you mean?" asked DJ.

"Are you guys a couple?"

DJ smiled. "Maybe . . ."

"You said you were just friends," said Taylor from the backseat.

"We *were*."

"I don't know why I believe you about anything," said Taylor. "You are such a flake."

115

"Why? Because I told you we were just friends?" DJ shook her head. "How was I supposed to know where the relationship was headed?"

Eliza chuckled. "Oh, DJ, you are a sly one."

"How's that?" asked DJ innocently.

Eliza laughed loudly. "You just are."

Then, just as they were about to merge onto the main road, DJ noticed a state trooper car parked nearby. "Look, Eliza," she said as one of the troopers waved his hand to motion them off to the side of the road.

"Oh, man," groaned Eliza. "I am so glad you're driving."

DJ was glad too, but she was also nervous. And for no explainable reason, she felt guilty. Maybe it was guilt by association.

"Afternoon," said the trooper, as the other cop motioned the Jeep that was coming up the road behind them to pull over too. "We're just doing a little Labor Day road check to make sure that no one is driving while under the influence." He looked down at DJ. "We've had some problems with alcohol down on this portion of beach."

She nodded without speaking. Suddenly her throat felt dry; maybe it was from the saltwater.

"Have you been drinking?"

"No, sir," said DJ. "Not at all. I mean except for soda."

"May I see your license, registration, and proof of insurance?"

"Sure." She reached for her bag which was wedged under the seat and Eliza got into the glove box for the other documents. DJ felt even more nervous as she searched in the Hermès bag for her wallet. Hopefully Taylor hadn't sabotaged her again. But, fortunately, her wallet was there and her license was right where it was supposed to be. She pulled it out and handed it, as well as the things that Eliza had found, to the policeman.

"This is my friend's car," said DJ, nodding to Eliza who cupped her hand in a little wave. "She was just letting me try it out."

"Do you mind getting out of the car?" he asked.

"Okay." She unbuckled the seat belt and got out.

"Do you mind walking for me?"

"Is this a sobriety test?" she asked.

"Sort of." He told her what to do and she obliged, walking back and forth along the sandy road, as well as some other things. It looked like Conner was getting pretty much the same drill. She even waved at him and he grinned and gave her a thumbs-up.

"Looks good," said the trooper as he handed her back the documents.

She smiled at him now. "You can even smell my breath if you want. Although it might smell like seawater since I swallowed about a quart a little while ago. But I honestly haven't been drinking. I'm not into that."

He laughed. "No, I won't need to smell your breath. You did just fine, Miss Lane. It's refreshing to see that some young folks are being responsible these days. Too often we find them after they've already blown it. Sometimes we're picking up the pieces at a wreck site."

She nodded. "Yeah, that would not be cool."

"Thanks for cooperating."

"Thank you," said DJ.

He smiled. "Now drive safe."

She got back into the car, buckled up, turned the key, put it into gear, turned on her left signal, and slowly pulled out and carefully drove.

"Whew," said Eliza. "You did great, DJ."

"Aren't you glad you let me drive?"

"Oh yeah." Eliza let out a sigh of relief. "Thanks, DJ." She reached over and patted her on the shoulder. "You're my new best friend."

Well, DJ wasn't so sure she wanted to be Eliza's best friend. At the same time there was a slice of satisfaction knowing that she was back in her good graces again. It was strange how quickly things could change. One moment, she's so humiliated that she's ready to call and beg her dad (a dad who really didn't want her) to see if she can go back and live with him. The next minute she's having a fantastic time, making new friends and paying volleyball. Then she gets put down so meanly that she literally jumps into the ocean and attempts to swim to England. And then, just minutes later, she's embracing a guy she really, really likes and experiencing her first kiss! Talk about a roller-coaster ride!

And now, here she was driving Eliza's gorgeous Porsche while Eliza is singing her praises and wanting to be her new best friend. Life really was crazy. Still, DJ knew these positive elements would probably come with a hefty price tag. She glanced in the rearview mirror just in time to catch Taylor scowling darkly, both her arms folded across her chest, and probably plotting her next devious act of revenge.

DJ remembered what Conner had said, and as ironic as it had seemed, maybe he was right. Maybe Taylor really was jealous of her. And maybe DJ had better start watching her backside a little bit better.

mixed bags

"Desiree," said Inez as the four girls came into the house. "Your grandmother told me to speak to you as soon as you got back."

"Is something wrong?" asked DJ as she followed Inez into Grandmother's office.

"The new girls are here." Inez had an unreadable expression. "Rhiannon will room with Taylor."

"Yes, I know that." DJ couldn't help but feel sorry for Rhiannon. How long would it be before Taylor would sink her claws into that poor girl? Just the fact that Rhiannon had absolutely no money, came from an unimpressive family, and owned no designer wardrobe would give Taylor plenty of ways to torment her.

But DJ knew that Rhiannon was strong. Even in the worst of circumstances, that girl seemed to come out of things okay. Like when she had to clean house just to make enough money to help her mom pay the rent, Rhiannon never complained. She told DJ once that her strength came from her faith in God. But DJ thought it was probably something more. Maybe it was simply because Rhiannon was a truly good person. Still, the thought of Rhiannon, the angel, rooming with Taylor, the devil ... well, it was a little disturbing.

"And Miss Atwood is here."

"Casey?" said DJ happily. It didn't escape her notice that Inez differentiated between Casey and Rhiannon. Just because Rhiannon had worked here, she didn't call her Miss Farley. But Casey was Miss Atwood. It figured.

"She's in your room."

"Is that it?" DJ felt impatient. "Is that all Grandmother wanted to tell me?"

"Well, uh, there is some concern over Miss Atwood."

"Concern?" DJ frowned. "Is Casey okay?"

"That's what's troubling your grandmother, Desiree. She said that Casey does not seem to be herself. I believe those were her words. And she's hoping that you can help."

"Help?"

"You know, just talk to your friend. Find out what's wrong."

"Why are you so sure that something's wrong?"

Inez shrugged. "I don't know. I'm talking for your grandmother."

"Where is she anyway?" demanded DJ. "She can't possibly still be napping at this hour."

"No. General Harding stopped by shortly after she got up. They went to town ... for ..."

"For drinks," DJ finished for her. "It figures. All the girls are here, and my grandmother is off drinking martinis with the general."

Inez chuckled. "I'm sure you can fill in for her, Desiree."

"Yeah, right." She shook her head. "I'm going to see Casey now."

DJ was curious as she went up the stairs. She wondered

what the problem with Casey could be. Maybe she was depressed. Or perhaps just worried about this move. She'd never been a girl to like change. DJ remembered when Casey's mom had painted her room mint green and replaced bedding and curtains while Casey had spent the weekend at DJ's house. It was kind of a like an episode on *While You Were Out*. DJ had thought it was great, but Casey had thrown a fit when she'd seen it. She'd said it wasn't her room anymore. She wanted her mom to change it back. But eventually she got used to it. DJ thought she even decided she liked it after awhile.

And surely, Casey would be happy to see DJ. They had been friends for, like, forever. And now they would be roommates. They could share secrets and create a life that was separate from the fashion-crazy world of Carter House. Maybe Casey would want to go out for volleyball. And DJ could tell her all about Conner and their first kiss. Casey would totally get that.

It seemed as if the playing field was leveling just now. DJ had felt like such an outsider since the other girls had arrived. Eliza, Taylor, and even Kriti were all from fairly wealthy families, totally into fashion, and a little on the snooty side. But now there was Rhiannon, who was poor by any standards, and Casey who was plain old middle class, and that placed DJ pretty much in the middle of this group. It seemed a good place to be.

"Casey?" said DJ as she opened the door to her room. There were bags and things littered about, as if someone had hurriedly dumped them and left. But the bathroom door was shut. "Casey?" she called again. "You in there?"

"Coming," said a grumpy-sounding voice.

"It's me, DJ!"

The door opened and a girl emerged. At least DJ thought

it was a girl. Her hair was cut short, and it was sticking up in all directions. She had on a black T-shirt with a skull on the front. And instead of the strawberry blonde hair that DJ remembered, this person's hair was jet black except for a section in the center that stuck straight up like a Mohawk and was dyed electric blue.

"Casey?"

The girl frowned. "You don't remember me?"

"Of course, I remember you. You just look different." Now DJ stared at the thick black circles of eyeliner that made Casey's brown eyes look very dark and rather raccoon-like.

"You have a problem with that?"

DJ cringed as she noticed that Casey also had a safety pin pierced through the edge of each of her eyebrows. "Ouch, didn't that hurt?"

"What?"

DJ pointed to a silver pin.

Casey shrugged. "Yeah, it hurt." Then she stuck out her tongue to reveal that it was pierced too. "That hurt more."

DJ frowned. "Then why did you do it?"

"Cuz I wanted to." Casey narrowed her eyes and turned away.

"Oh . . ." It was all sinking in now. This was why DJ's grandmother had been upset, why she'd told Inez to talk to DJ. Perhaps even why she'd gone off to consume martinis with the general. But, surely, Grandmother didn't expect DJ to sort this all out.

"You look shocked," said Casey as she flopped onto the window seat, folding her arms across her chest. That spot had previously been DJ's favorite place to sit in the room. She felt slightly disoriented.

"I'm a little surprised."

122

"Well, get over it."

Now DJ sat down at the foot of her bed, across from Casey. "So, was your mom okay with all this? I mean aren't your parents kind of conservative?"

"That's an understatement. They are so uptight and paranoid over appearances that they've been totally freaked. That's why I'm here, you know. They're too embarrassed to have me around anymore. They quit making me go to church with them when I pierced my eyebrows. Just because they were so mortified." She laughed. "It's one way to get out of going to church."

DJ nodded with what she hoped was an expression of empathy. And she could actually understand this, although probably not from Casey's perspective. The fact was, although she would never admit it, she might be embarrassed to be seen with Casey too. "That's too bad," she said simply.

"So, here I am." Casey held out her hands as if she were helpless, but this gesture revealed a dark tattoo-like image on her wrist.

"Did you get tattoos too?"

"No, not permanently anyway. Although I plan to, if I can get some cash together." She pushed up the sleeve on her left arm to reveal a long black dragon, complete with claws and fire and a spiky tail. "I drew this on the flight out here. The woman next to me was totally disgusted." She laughed. "Oh, she didn't say anything—she didn't need to—I could just tell."

"You're a good artist," observed DJ. Okay, it wasn't her style of art, but it was well-done. "Did you meet the other girl that arrived today? Rhiannon?"

Casey groaned and rolled her eyes. "Give me a break. That girl actually started preaching at me. She was telling me how the dragon was a biblical sign in the book of Revelation and blah, blah, blah … I actually had to tell her to shut up."

"You told her to shut up?"

"Yes. Then I told her I was practically raised in a church, and that there was nothing she could tell me that I hadn't already heard."

"Oh."

"And that shut her up," said Casey.

"Well, Rhiannon is pretty committed to her church."

"What an idiot."

"She's actually kind of nice," said DJ.

"You know her?"

"Yes. She did housekeeping for my grandmother last spring. Her mom was in this crummy divorce and not doing too well. Rhiannon was trying to earn enough money for them to stay in their house. But they had to move anyway."

"Oh …"

"And, according to Rhiannon, her church was the only thing she could count on. Her mom had a, uh, a problem … and Rhiannon found comfort in going to church. She'd only been going there for a year."

"She went to church of her own free will?" Casey asked.

"Yeah. Her mom didn't want anything to do with it," said DJ.

"That is weird," said Casey.

DJ wanted to point out that it wasn't quite as weird as Casey's dark transformation. Now that was weird.

"So, if Rhiannon is so poor that they couldn't stay in their house, why is she even here? I thought the Carter House was just for rich witch girls."

DJ considered this. She knew that her grandmother didn't want this to be known, but how could they keep Rhiannon's poverty a secret. "My grandmother has an arrangement with Rhiannon's mom."

Casey kind of laughed. "Maybe Rhiannon's mom sold her into slavery to your grandmother, and you just don't know it yet."

Surprisingly, DJ almost wanted to defend her grandmother. But she didn't. "This is my bed," she said, getting up to remove some of the things from the other bed. Things that Eliza had given her this morning. She wasn't sure what to do with them, or if she even wanted to keep them after all that had transpired. Still, she and Eliza had seemed okay when it was all said and done. In some ways, Eliza seemed safer than her old friend Casey right now. Was she really going to share her room with a girl who looked like she might sneak out to worship Satan in the middle of the night?

"You've changed too," said Casey.

She could feel Casey watching her as she dumped the pile of clothes onto her own bed and began to sort them. "I guess we all change," DJ said as she held up a cool pair of jeans. They were much better looking than her old favorites. Hopefully they would fit. "Change is just part of growing up."

"Did your grandma tell you that my parents were going to send me to boot camp?"

"Boot camp? Like in the army?"

"No, like for juvenile delinquents."

DJ turned around and studied Casey now. "Does that mean you're a criminal?" She actually did resemble a juvenile delinquent.

Casey shrugged. "Guess it depends on how you define *criminal*. I've broken the law, but who hasn't?"

DJ considered this. She didn't think she'd ever broken the law. Although she had felt guilty when stopped by the police today. Although she hadn't been drinking, she was with others who had been. Being underaged, they had broken the law. Did that mean she was in the wrong just because she was with them?

"I really need a shower," she told Casey as she held out her still damp and saltwater-soaked blouse. "I took a little dip in the ocean—with my clothes on—and it's feeling kinda gross now."

Casey waved her hand. "Go ahead. Don't let me stop you."

"I'm sure we'll have all kinds of time to catch up," said DJ in a voice that sounded falsely cheerful. "Sharing a room and all." Then she grabbed up a couple of things from the pile of Eliza hand-me-downs and took them into the bathroom with her. As she showered, DJ remembered how she had planned to tell Casey all about Conner and her salty first kiss. For some reason, she knew that talk wasn't going to happen now. She had no idea what had happened to Casey or why she wanted to look like that—why she wanted to stick safety pins through her eyebrows or a hole in her tongue—but it made no sense. It was like self-inflicted pain. Why would someone do that?

DJ had experienced enough pain during the past few years, starting with her parents' divorce when she was thirteen, followed up by her mom's death just a year ago, and finally being rejected by her dad in exchange for his new family. All that was enough to make her want to avoid pain for a long, long time, if not forever. Even the painful emotional events from the past couple of days, which were small in comparison to the rest of her life, were more than she cared to go through again.

She dried off, and then tried on several of the pieces Eliza had given to her. The jeans seemed to fit pretty well. She noticed that the brand was called True Religion, and she had to wonder what was up with that. But the jeans were cool, and from what she could see from the mirror above the sink, they looked good on her. After trying on a couple of things, she topped the jeans with a pale yellow blouse bearing a label that said Tocca. This didn't mean anything to her either. But she decided to try to remember these names. After all, it wasn't that big of a deal. And if she had to live with girls like Eliza and Kriti, and even the despicable Taylor, it wouldn't hurt to learn to speak their language. It didn't mean that she was like them, but simply that she was trying to get along.

Okay, she knew this shifting of position had something to do with her new roommate and old friend. And she wasn't even sure why that was, but for some reason it suddenly seemed important. It also seemed important to look her best, and that seemed to have to do with Conner. She looked at herself in the mirror, remembering how he had called her beautiful. But that was after she'd been sweating and swimming and probably looked somewhat natural. She still had some of the cosmetics that Eliza had helped her with this morning. And she did apply some of the moisturizer to her face, but other than a little mascara and lip gloss, she thought maybe she was good to go. Not that she necessarily expected to see Conner tonight, but after the talk of movies, she thought there was a slim chance.

"That's better," said DJ as she emerged from the bathroom.

Casey frowned from where she was still slumped in the window seat. "Your boyfriend called."

DJ blinked. "What?"

"Your boyfriend. He called on your cell. I heard it ringing, and I went ahead and answered it for you."

"Oh." DJ glanced over to her Hermès with the phone now placed on top of it. "And?"

"And he said to call."

"Okay." But DJ didn't want to call Conner while Casey was listening. And yet, she didn't want to make Casey feel bad.

"Aren't you going to call Lover Boy back?"

This made DJ mad. But she didn't show it. Instead she called Conner. "Hey," she said. "I hear you called."

"Yeah, who was that?"

"That's Casey Atwood," she told him, glancing over to where Casey was pretending to ignore this conversation. "She's an old friend, and now she's my roommate." It was easy to say this on the phone, but it would be tricky when she introduced Casey to Conner face-to-face. Hopefully she could warn him first. And yet she knew that he was a good guy; he wouldn't make Casey feel bad. No, that would be for Taylor to do.

"So, are you still up for a movie tonight? Harry talked to Eliza and she wants to go out."

"Yeah, that sounds good."

"Do you want to invite your friend too?"

"Sure. Do you know if the other girls are going? Taylor and Kriti?"

He chuckled. "Meaning is there a way we can keep Taylor a safe distance from you?"

"Something like that."

"I don't know. But if they are coming, we might need more than two cars."

"I guess it could be kind of tight."

"I could bring my truck."

"You have a truck?" For some reason DJ was imagining Conner driving a semi just now.

"It's an old Chevy pickup that my dad's been helping me to fix up."

"Cool. I'd love to see it."

"Well, find out if all the girls are going, and if we need more room I'll bring it by."

"Okay, I'll let you know."

"Oh, yeah, the movie starts at eight-thirty."

So DJ hung up and then turned to Casey. "Want to go to a movie tonight?"

"With you and Lover Boy? Yeah, right."

"No, I think the other girls are going too. We talked about it at the beach today."

"I don't know ..." Casey looked kind of lost just now.

"Come on," urged DJ. "It's better than hanging out here with my grandmother."

Casey rolled her eyes.

"How about if I check with the others?" said DJ. "If everyone is going, maybe you'll want to come too?"

"Oh, yeah, because I'm such a joiner. I just love doing what everyone else is doing. It's so unique."

DJ peered at this strange girl who used to be like a sister. "Look, I don't know what's going on with you, Casey, but you've obviously changed. And I do want to hear the details. But I don't need you laying into me right now. I've already got my hands full with one girl who hates my guts. I'd like to think that you're still my friend."

Casey brightened now. "Who hates your guts?"

DJ sighed. "Taylor. She's one of my grandmother's protégés and the meanest girl I've ever met."

"Cool."

DJ frowned. "Cool?"

"Not cool that she's being mean to you. But at least she's not afraid to be herself. She's probably not just a cookie cutter, rich witch, fashion goddess."

"Don't be too sure about that." DJ glanced at the clock.

"If we're going to the movie, we need to get this nailed. I'll go check with the others."

However, as she left her room, she planned to check only with Eliza and Kriti. If they wanted to confront Lioness Taylor in her den, they were more than welcome. But DJ had had enough of Taylor for one day.

13

mixed bags

"I don't want to go out tonight," said Kriti, who was sitting on the window seat with a thick book in her lap. Her hair was still damp from her shower, and she was wearing an elegant pair of purple silk pajamas and looking very much like an Indian princess.

"Oh." DJ looked over to where Eliza was fussing with her hair. "How about you?"

"I'm in," said Eliza.

"Why don't you guys just make it a double date?" suggested Kriti. Then she gave DJ a slightly wicked smile. "Unless you're enthused about having Taylor with you. I'm sure she'll liven things up."

"Kriti's right," said Eliza. "This should be a double date."

"Will you tell Taylor?"

"Sure. You call the guys. But we need to get going."

So DJ went back to her room and explained the plan to Casey who acted as if she could care less. "Whatever."

"You're sure?" said DJ, suddenly feeling guilty for leaving her old friend behind. Not only that, DJ suddenly realized that she hadn't even said hello to Rhiannon yet. Still, she knew that would mean seeing Taylor, and she just wasn't up for that yet.

"Yeah, I'm fine. I haven't even unpacked yet, and I've got a bunch of email to catch up on anyway. Just go, okay?"

"Okay." So DJ called Conner. The guys were on their way over, and she was just going to get Eliza when she heard Inez calling her.

"Desiree," said Inez, coming up the stairs. "Mrs. Carter wishes to see you in her office."

"Just a minute." DJ tapped on Eliza's door.

"She already went downstairs," said Kriti. Then she smiled at DJ. "Have fun!"

"Thanks. Enjoy your book. What is it anyway?"

"*Gone With the Wind*. I found it in the library downstairs."

"Is it good?"

Kriti nodded with wide eyes. "Yes, really good."

"Maybe I'll read it next."

"Cool. We can have a mini book club."

Then DJ took off downstairs. Hopefully, whatever Grandmother wanted could be handled quickly because the guys would be here any minute.

"I need to talk to Grandmother," DJ told Eliza who was waiting in the foyer.

"Taylor was just talking to her," said Eliza as she checked her hair in the mirror.

DJ nodded, hurrying toward the office. "I'll be right back."

"Desiree," said Grandmother. "Close the door behind you, please."

DJ shut the door. "We need to keep this quick. Eliza and I are going out tonight."

"No, Desiree, you are not."

132

"What?" DJ stared at Grandmother. This was the first time her grandmother had ever told her no about anything, well, other than about her appearance, which she protested on a regular basis. But when it came to coming and going, Grandmother had never really seemed to care.

"You are not going out tonight."

"Why not?"

"Because we are having a meeting."

"A meeting?"

"Yes. Taylor expressed concerns over how things are going in Carter House."

"Taylor?" DJ blinked.

"Yes. She feels we are too unstructured, and that the rules are not clear."

"The girls all signed a contract, Grandmother, the rules were on it." DJ also wanted to add that Taylor was systematically breaking the rules.

"Nevertheless, I think Taylor is right. We need to have a meeting." Grandmother smiled. "Let's not call it a meeting. It will be more of a social gathering."

"But Eliza and I were —"

"Yes, please, inform Eliza that there is a change in plans."

"But —"

"And let the other girls know that we will have a meeting in the living room at eight o'clock. Refreshments will be provided."

"Like carrot and celery sticks," said DJ.

Grandmother actually laughed, which DJ figured could only be the result of her martini afternoon with the general. "Oh, Desiree, you're such a funny child."

DJ glared at her grandmother now. "I just want you to

133

know I think this is totally unfair. Eliza and I had plans, and now you're ruining everything."

"Desiree," Grandmother's eyes narrowed now and her tone grew serious. "It will do no harm to put off the young men for one evening. Tell them you must postpone your date until tomorrow night. They will simply conclude that you and Eliza are well worth the wait."

DJ considered this. Maybe Grandmother had a point. Still, it was aggravating to think that this was another small victory for Taylor. DJ had no doubts that Taylor had manipulated this stupid meeting just to keep Eliza and DJ under her thumb.

"All right," DJ finally agreed. "But you better not pull something like this tomorrow night."

"Desiree," said Grandmother just as DJ was leaving. "Please, wait a minute."

DJ paused by the door as her grandmother came over and peered curiously at her. "No ball cap?" She cupped DJ's chin in her hand and tipped her face up. "A touch of makeup?" Her expression grew hopeful. "You might just be turning into a lovely young woman after all."

DJ was surprised by the unexpected compliment. "Uh, thanks."

Grandmother picked up a strand of her hair and studied it. "I could get you an appointment with Val ... perhaps a trim and some highlights?"

DJ shrugged. "Yeah, maybe."

Grandmother smiled now. "Run and tell your young men that you and Eliza have other plans for this evening."

DJ went out to see that Eliza and the "young men" were out on the porch, waiting for her. Conner's eyes lit up when she joined them.

"Ready?" he asked hopefully.

"Bad news," she announced.

"What?" asked Eliza.

"Taylor ..." DJ shook her head. "I swear that girl wants to destroy me."

"What did she do?" demanded Conner.

So DJ explained Taylor's "concern" over the lack of structure in Carter House. "She convinced my grandmother to have a meeting tonight so that she can go over all the rules with the girls."

Eliza laughed. "So that Taylor can figure a new way to break them?"

"Exactly."

"Why don't you tell your grandmother the truth?" suggested Conner. "Tell her that Taylor smokes and drinks and lies and —"

"The thought has crossed my mind," admitted DJ. "But my grandmother is so smitten by Taylor's mom's celebrity that I'm afraid she'd put up with almost anything to keep Taylor here."

"And she might settle down," said Eliza. "Especially if the other girls put some pressure on her."

"Anyway," DJ sighed. "Grandmother said that Eliza and I can go out tomorrow night, if you guys want to ..."

"Sure, we want to," said Harry as he eyed Eliza.

"Of course," agreed Conner, reaching for DJ's hand and giving it a warm squeeze that sent happy tingles down her spine.

"Sorry about this," she told him.

"It's not your fault." His eyes looked even bluer now than they had in the ocean.

"Hey, we could still make it to the guy movie," said Harry suddenly.

Conner grinned. "Yeah, we were fairly sure you girls wouldn't want to see this particular film. It's a war movie and supposed to be full of some pretty graphic violence."

"Blood and guts and gore," added Harry, like that was a good thing.

"Not exactly my cup of tea," said Eliza.

"Or mine," added DJ.

"You boys go and enjoy." Eliza smiled up at Harry, and he leaned down and gave her a peck on the cheek. Then Conner, looking slightly uncomfortable, like he was unsure as to how DJ would react, followed suit. They made a little more small talk and then finally said good-bye. Eliza and DJ watched as the guys got into Harry's Jeep, and they waved from the porch before they went back inside.

"This is so unfair," said DJ as she closed the door.

"Oh, I was kind of tired anyway," admitted Eliza.

"Well, my grandmother suggested that it might do our 'young men' some good to wait for us." DJ snickered.

Eliza chuckled as they went up the stairs. "I think Mrs. Carter might have that just about right. We wouldn't want them to think we're overly eager."

DJ wasn't so sure about that. She was eager to spend more time with Conner, and she was mad at Taylor for spoiling it. The mere thought that she could be with Conner right now on her way to do something fun versus being stuck here with a bunch of girls ... well, it was extremely aggravating!

"I'm supposed to let the other girls know about the meeting," she said at the landing.

"I'll tell Kriti."

"Wanna tell Taylor too?"

"I would assume that she already knows."

"Yeah, right, but I should probably make sure Rhiannon knows too." DJ got an idea. "Have you met Rhiannon yet?"

"No, she was in the bathroom when I told Taylor that only you and I were going out tonight."

"You mean before Taylor went whining to my grandmother?"

Eliza nodded.

"So, do you want to meet Rhiannon? She's really nice."

"Sure."

So both Eliza and DJ knocked on Taylor's door.

Taylor opened it. "What do you two want?" she asked in a bored tone.

"Obviously you know about the special meeting," said DJ. "We want to talk to Rhiannon."

"DJ?" cried a happy voice. Rhiannon burst out of the room and hugged DJ. "I'm so happy to see you!"

"Me too," said DJ.

"Come in," said Rhiannon, opening the door wider as she pulled the two of them in. Taylor sat in one of the easy chairs and pretended to read a fashion rag, but DJ could tell she was watching the three of them.

DJ introduced Rhiannon to Eliza. "And Rhiannon is a talented artist," she told her.

"Really? What kind of art?"

"Oh, just about everything," said Rhiannon happily. "Not that I'm any good, but I just like doing it."

"She *is* good," declared DJ. "When school starts, you'll see an amazing mural that she painted in the courtyard last year."

"With Bradford Wale's help," said Rhiannon. "I couldn't have done it without him."

"Bradford's mother is a professional artist," said DJ.

"Have you heard of Gabrielle Bruyere?"

"It sounds familiar," said Eliza with real interest.

"I haven't met her yet," admitted DJ, "but Rhiannon showed me some of her work at The Mockingbird."

"What's The Mockingbird?"

"The best gallery in Crescent Cove," said Rhiannon. "My goal is to get into it before I turn thirty."

"Oh, you'll be in it before you turn twenty," said DJ.

"You're too sweet," said Rhiannon.

"You're all too sweet," said Taylor with disgust. "Can't you take your little chit-chat session somewhere else? This is, after all, a fairly large house."

"Oh, sorry," said Rhiannon.

"Don't mind her," said DJ. "She's a perennial grump."

"Thanks." Taylor growled.

"Let's get out of here," said DJ. "Grandmother said she's serving refreshments at the meeting tonight. Maybe we should get down there and see if it's anything better than veggie sticks and nonfat dip."

"I'm craving kettle corn," said Eliza.

"I'm craving ice cream," said Rhiannon.

"I'm craving privacy," snapped Taylor.

"You got it," said DJ as she opened the door and led the others out, firmly shutting the door behind them.

"Poor Rhiannon," said Eliza, patting her on the back.

"Why?" asked Rhiannon.

"Have you notice that you're rooming with a witch?" said DJ.

Rhiannon just smiled. "God works in mysterious ways, DJ."

"What's that supposed to mean?" asked Eliza as they went down the stairs.

"It means that I think God put me with Taylor for a reason."

"What kind of reason?" demanded DJ.

"I think she just needs someone to love her."

"Wow," said Eliza. "Are you for real? Or are you like a saint or an angel or something?"

Rhiannon laughed. "Trust me, I'm totally human. And a year ago, I probably would've freaked over being stuck with a girl like Taylor."

"So what's the difference now?" asked Eliza with real curiosity.

"God."

"But how?"

"Well, I never believed in God before," said Rhiannon as they went into the living room to find that, according to Grandmother's promise, there on the big, square coffee table were refreshments. And besides the typical veggie sticks and nonfat dip, there were also pretzels and tortilla chips (most assuredly they were baked ones with no trans fats, but chips nonetheless) and a big bowl of homemade salsa. "But I hit a hard place," continued Rhiannon, "and when I turned to God, he was definitely there for me."

They sat down around the table and began snacking.

"What kind of hard place?" asked Eliza.

Rhiannon glanced at DJ now, as if unsure of how much she should tell. DJ suspected that her grandmother had told Rhiannon to keep her past under wraps. Still, DJ felt it was Rhiannon's business.

"Rhiannon's mom has had some problems," said DJ simply.

"My mom is a drug addict," said Rhiannon.

"I'm sorry," said Eliza in a tone that sounded genuinely sympathetic.

"Thanks." Rhiannon took a carrot stick. "She wasn't always

like that. But when my dad left, my mom felt really bad about herself ... rejected and everything. She decided she should lose weight."

"So she started taking drugs?" asked Eliza.

"Yeah, she started with diet pills ... and it escalated."

"That's too bad."

"I tried to keep things together," said Rhiannon, "but it got harder and harder."

"Yeah, Rhiannon was working to help cover their expenses," said DJ. "She was acting more like the mom than her mom."

"That had to be hard."

"It was." Then Rhiannon smiled. "But it was what got me to search for God. I needed help. My mom was into astrology and stuff ... and I could see there were no real answers there. A friend at school kept inviting me to go to church things with her. I kept making excuses. Then one day I just said okay. And all I can say is that God made himself real to me. I asked Jesus into my heart and became a Christian, and everything began to change."

"Everything except your mom," added DJ.

"I guess I mean everything *inside* of me," said Rhiannon. "It's like I started to become a new person." She looked at DJ now. "Seriously, DJ, you didn't know me before this happened. But I wasn't that much different than Taylor back then. I was dark and depressed and angry."

"No way!" said Eliza.

"Way!" Rhiannon laughed.

"Wow!" DJ tried to wrap her head around this. "That just does not compute. I cannot imagine you being even a little bit like Taylor."

"Ask Bradford," said Rhiannon. "Or Emery, the girl who invited me to her church."

"And how long ago was this big transformation anyway?" asked DJ, still feeling a little skeptical. Not that Rhiannon would lie, but it was hard to believe.

"Not quite a year. I gave my heart to the Lord in October."

Just then the other girls started coming into the room and the conversation switched gears. Still, DJ couldn't help but wonder at Rhiannon's strange story. She simply couldn't imagine the sweet, kindhearted Rhiannon being anything like the self-centered and mean Taylor. It was like saying day was night or white was black. It just made absolutely no sense.

14

mixed bags

"Welcome to the Carter House," said Mrs. Carter as she entered the room like she was gliding down a fashion runway in New York. DJ noticed that her grandmother had changed her outfit. She was now wearing a cream-colored silk pantsuit that sort of flowed as she walked. This was stylishly combined with some large pieces of very expensive-looking gold jewelry. She had touched up her makeup and even had on a pair of gold metallic sandals. Even DJ had to admit that, with her platinum hair, expressive eyes, and high cheekbones, she was rather striking—at least for a woman her age.

The girls became quiet as they watched her position herself in front of the fireplace, placing some things on the mantel. "I'm so glad you're all here now," she continued. "I think we're going to have a wonderful year at the Carter House. I have so much planned for you, and when we're done, I think you will all blossom into the beautiful young women that you are meant to be."

Then she gave a brief—okay not so brief—history of her illustrious fashion career, starting from when she was first discovered. "I wasn't much older than you girls, almost eighteen and a senior in high school. My parents were shocked when a family friend who was working in the fashion industry suggested that I might have what it took to model. I was taller than most girls; five nine back then was considered quite gangly for a girl. And I also had a good figure. Interestingly enough, models back then were heavier than nowadays. Photographers were looking for girls with curves." She smiled. "But that was the fifties. Times have changed, haven't they?"

The girls sort of nodded like they understood. And DJ had noticed already that both Eliza and Taylor seemed to be constantly watching what they ate. Even tonight, DJ hadn't seen Eliza eat more than a few veggie sticks, and she didn't even dip them. For that matter, it seemed that she, Kriti, and Rhiannon were the only ones "indulging" in the chips and salsa. Well, whatever. DJ wasn't into that. And it appalled her to see how emaciated some of the girls in the fashion magazines looked. No way could those stick girls do sports. They wouldn't have the stamina. That whole skin-and-bones look just didn't appeal to her.

"But even when I was accepted at a top-notch modeling agency, my father put his foot down," Grandmother continued. "He thought modeling was scandalous. But my mother was more open-minded. She liked the idea. And finally, we worked it out so that both Mother and I could live in New York where we gave the modeling scene a whirl." She laughed. "And, oh my, did we whirl. My parents had no idea that I would be such a success."

DJ had heard most of this before, but she was somewhat impressed at how her grandmother was able to hold most of the girls' attention, almost as if she really were someone famous. For that matter, maybe she was, or had been back in her day. All the girls were listening and watching her as if they really thought she was something. Well, except for Casey who was sitting off by herself and looked as if she wanted to be anywhere but here.

Finally, DJ was curious as to whether or not her grandmother really intended to go over the rules as she had suggested. It seemed that tonight's meeting was all about her, and after an hour, she suspected that everyone was getting a little bored. Or maybe it was just her.

"Excuse me," said DJ, when there was a brief pause. "Are you going to go over the house rules, Grandmother?"

Her grandmother smiled. "Yes, thank you for reminding me." She took the small stack of papers on the mantle and handed it to DJ. "Can you give each of the girls one of these?"

DJ distributed the papers, which looked like they were from the contract.

"But before we go over this, I think we should make sure that everyone has met. We had two new girls arrive while the rest of you were at the beach." Then she introduced Rhiannon and Casey. "Perhaps we should all go around and say a bit about ourselves. You've heard part of my story ... now it's time to hear yours." She seemed to consider this. "Perhaps you could tell us your name, where you are from, and what you expect to get out of your stay here." She nodded to DJ. "Desiree will start."

DJ controlled herself from rolling her eyes. "I'm DJ," she said.

"Please stand, *Desiree*. And face the audience."

DJ let out a big breath, but obliged. "My grandmother, Mrs. Carter, insists on calling me Desiree, but I go by DJ. DJ Lane. My real name is *Desiree Jeannette*." She used an authentic French accent, which made some of the girls—not Taylor or Casey—chuckle. "It was because my mother spent some time

145

in France, and she must've thought she was going to have a lovely little French girl. Instead she got a tomboy. Anyway, I lived in California ... outside of San Francisco ... until my mom died. Then I lived with my dad. Now I'm here." She looked at her grandmother. "What was the other question?"

Even her grandmother looked stumped.

"What do you expect to get from your stay here?" offered Kriti, who had obviously been paying attention.

"Oh, yeah. What do I want to get?" She looked at her grandmother. "Maybe some peace and quiet."

The girls laughed. Well, except for the two grouches. Casey and Taylor looked like they might get along.

"Thank you, Desiree, that will do." Grandmother pointed to Eliza now.

"I'm Eliza Wilton, and I'm from Louisville, although my parents are living in France right now. And I hope that I will make some new friends, and maybe I'll learn to be as fashionable as Mrs. Carter by the time I'm done."

"Thank you, dear," said Grandmother.

Then Kriti took a turn, explaining how she was originally from India and more recently New York City, where her parents still lived. "I hope to get an exceptional education, make excellent grades, and get accepted into an outstanding college."

Casey made a sound that was a cross between a grunt and a laugh.

"How about you, Casey?" said Grandmother with a narrowed gaze. All the girls turned around and looked at Casey now. DJ had a feeling that Casey's days here were numbered, maybe even in the single digits.

Casey shrugged. "I'm Casey Atwood. I lived in Sacramento.

And I don't have the slightest idea what I'm supposed to get out of being here."

Grandmother cleared her throat. "Yes, we'll see what we can do about that, dear." She smiled at Taylor. "Go ahead, Taylor."

"I'm Taylor Mitchell. I lived in LA with my mom who's a singer. I came here to learn to be a proper young lady." Taylor said this with a completely straight face, and DJ felt relatively sure that her grandmother actually bought it.

"Taylor's being modest," said Grandmother with a proud expression, "Her mother is Eva Perez, the internationally re-nowned recording artist." Now she nodded to Rhiannon. "And our latest addition to our little family."

Rhiannon stood. "I'm Rhiannon Farley. I used to live in Crescent Cove, but then we moved to New Jersey to live with my aunt for a while. I consider myself very blessed to be back here now. And I hope to make the most of my time in the Carter House. I would love to learn to be more fashionable and refined. I've admired Mrs. Carter and her sense of style for several years. And I absolutely love designing clothes as well as other forms of art. I think being here is going to be a great experience."

Grandmother smiled. "Thank you, Rhiannon. Thank all of you. I just know that you girls are all going to be close friends—almost like sisters. I never had the opportunity to be in a sorority when I was young. I was too busy modeling and traveling. But I imagine this will be somewhat like that experi-ence. I realize that you girls are a bit younger than college stu-dents, but I expect you to conduct yourselves with maturity and respectability. That is the beauty of being a Carter House girl. You will stand out in the community as a girl who's committed to excellence, whose future is bright." She beamed at all of them.

DJ glanced around the room, wondering if anyone else felt like gagging just now, but the girls—other than Casey who looked like she'd like to throw something—all appeared to be on the same page. Although it was hard to tell with Taylor. DJ was ninety-nine percent certain this was simply an act. In fact she decided that, although Casey was fairly irritating, she preferred Casey's outright rebellious attitude compared to Taylor's hypocritical pretenses. At least everyone would know where Casey stood. Taylor would be the wild card.

Grandmother was still droning on. DJ wondered how much there could possibly be to say about this, but then she decided perhaps she should tune in a little better. Just in case there was a test afterward.

"And I know that you will all make me proud of you." Grandmother paused to reach for the things that she'd set on the mantel earlier. "However, it has been brought to my attention by a concerned girl that perhaps I need to clarify some things. As you all know I've tried to keep the rules simple, and you've all signed your contracts, but perhaps we should go over the rules more carefully again." She put on her reading glasses, unfolded a piece of paper, and then cleared her throat and read.

"All girls must attend school, maintain above-average grades, and respect the school district rules.

All girls must respect house curfew, which, unless otherwise agreed upon, is nine o'clock on school nights and eleven o'clock on non-school nights.

All girls are welcome to use the public areas of the house (living room, library, dining room, kitchen, and observatory) until ten o'clock on school nights and midnight on non-school nights.

All girls will refrain from smoking, drinking, or any form of substance abuse or other illegal activity.

148

All girls will refrain from unsavory speech, swearing, and general crudeness.

All girls will maintain their appearances and practice good etiquette at all times.

All girls will treat each other with respect.

All girls will conduct themselves with modesty and respectability both in private and public.

All girls will be responsible for their personal belongings and keep their bedrooms relatively neat.

All girls are expected to participate in fashion, etiquette, and style training sessions.

Any girl who breaks these rules is subject to loss of privileges and possible expulsion from the Carter House."

"Any questions?" asked Grandmother as she removed her glasses.

"Some of those rules seem pretty subjective to me," said Casey in a challenging tone.

"For instance?" Grandmother gave Casey her most intimidating stare.

"Like what does *maintain their appearances* mean?"

"It means Carter House girls will practice good hygiene, use good fashion sense, and dress neatly and cleanly and respectably."

"According to who?"

Grandmother stood straighter, holding her chin out. "According to me, Casey. This is, after all, *my* house. If you do not like the rules, no one is forcing you to remain here. We are not a detention facility. We are here to teach young ladies how to conduct themselves with dignity and in a way that will give them a cutting edge with all the challenges of life."

"All the *challenges of life*?" Casey laughed as she shook her head. "Do you have any idea what you're talking about?"

"Perhaps this is a discussion we should conduct privately, Casey."

"Yeah, maybe so." Casey didn't look exactly thrilled with this suggestion. DJ suspected Casey would prefer keeping it public. But then Grandmother wouldn't want the discomfort that would go along with that.

"Are there any other questions?"

No one raised a hand.

"So, I think that covers it. If any of you have questions in the future, you know that I am here for you, girls. And, of course, I'm happy to speak to you privately if necessary. I hope that you'll all be happy here, and I encourage your independence. I hope that you will respect yourselves and that you will respect the rules of the house. Thank you and good night."

And then, as dramatically as she entered, Grandmother glided out of the room in a graceful exit.

"How old is she anyway?" whispered Eliza. "I was just doing the math, and if she modeled in the fifties ... she'd be like in her seventies, wouldn't she?"

"No way," said Rhiannon. "She doesn't look much older than my mom."

DJ considered this. Rhiannon's mom didn't look too great anyway. "It's just because she keeps herself up," said DJ. "And she gets work done, you know."

"Even so," said Eliza. "My grandma is in her sixties and she looks way older than your grandma."

"You are all so freaking superficial," said Casey from where she was still sitting in the back of the room. "Do you honestly think that the world is going to bow down to you because you wear expensive clothes and have your hair done in the latest stupid style?"

150

The girls turned around to look at Casey now. There was such a drastic difference between everyone here and Casey. If DJ had felt like odd girl out before, Casey was going to be even more of a misfit.

"Well, why don't you tell us a little about your look," said Taylor as she stood and went closer. She put her hand on her chin and peered down at Casey as if she were an insect in a jar. "Are you supposed to be Goth? Or perhaps you're a rock star wannabe? Or maybe you're just a freak who can't fit in so she decided to drop out."

Casey stood now, facing Taylor with arms at her side, but fists curled as if she were about to punch her. "None of your business, *witch*," she seethed.

"Come on, you guys," said Rhiannon. She hopped up from the couch and went over to stand next to them. "We're all different. Can't we just respect our differences? I don't think Mrs. Carter wants us all to conform ourselves into mirror images of each other. I mean, look at me, I don't have expensive clothes. I can't afford them, but even if I could, I don't want them. I'd rather express my uniqueness by wearing my own designs."

Taylor turned and frowned at Rhiannon. "Yeah, that's fairly obvious." Taylor turned to the other girls and laughed. "I couldn't believe it when I saw what she was unpacking tonight. I thought I'd died and gone to hell and it was a thrift store."

DJ wanted to tell Taylor that she wished she would go to hell. But she had a feeling that would offend Rhiannon. And right now DJ had more respect for Rhiannon than anyone else in the room. Okay, she was weird. And DJ didn't really get it. But she had to admire the girl's bravery.

15

mixed bags

By Saturday morning, the Carter House felt like a pot that had been left on the stove too long. DJ expected it to boil over at any moment. For that reason, she was trying to lie low. Casey, who had missed breakfast, seemed even grouchier than last night. And she wasn't budging from their bedroom, where she was sitting on the window seat, playing a computer game that involved guns and screaming and made DJ feel as if she wanted to throw the laptop out the window. DJ had sought a haven in Eliza and Kriti's room, which seemed about the safest place, but after an hour or so, she was worried she might wear out her welcome. So it was that she was downstairs when her grandmother found her.

"Desiree," said Grandmother with enthusiasm. "I was just looking for you."

"Why?" she asked with suspicion.

"You are a lucky girl today."

"How's that?"

"I just spoke to Val, and he had a cancellation for his eleven o'clock appointment. I told him to save it for you." She reached out and fingered a strand of DJ's hair. "You really have good hair, Desiree. I think Val will have no problems."

"But I—"

"No, buts, dear. I gave Val instructions; all you need to do is show up and leave it to him. And it's nearly eleven now, so you better run along."

"What if it doesn't turn—?"

"Really, dear, no worries. Val has done this literally thousands of times. He's a pro. It's all set up. He'll simply put it on my bill. All you need to do is show up, and he'll take care of you."

DJ wasn't so sure. She hadn't had much experience with hair salons. In the past, she'd always just worn her hair long, and when it needed trimming, her mother had done it. Just having Eliza putting that stuff on it yesterday had been unsettling, but the idea of a stranger doing something to her hair, a man even, was pretty scary. "So you can promise me that my hair won't fall out, and that I'll like it?" asked DJ.

Her grandmother smiled in a way that wasn't quite convincing. "Of course, you'll like it, Desiree."

"You'll like what?" asked Eliza as she came down the stairs.

"Oh, Eliza," said Grandmother happily. "You're just the one I need. Please, encourage my granddaughter that getting her hair highlighted is nothing whatsoever to be afraid of."

So Eliza gave DJ just about the same little speech she'd given her yesterday. "And if it'll make you feel better, I'll come along with you. I'd like to see what's in town anyway."

"That's perfect," said Grandmother. "In fact, I have a wonderful idea, Eliza. Why don't you help Desiree pick out some new clothes for school? I've been trying to get her to do some shopping with me all summer, but it's been like pulling teeth. I'll bet she wouldn't mind going with you."

"That's a great idea," said Eliza. "But where does one shop in this town?"

So Grandmother gave her directions to the closest mall. "But, be forewarned, Eliza, this is a small town. Do not expect too much."

Then Grandmother gave DJ some cash as well as her Macy's credit card. "Not that I'm a Macy's fan," she said to Eliza in a confidential tone. "But sometimes I get rather desperate, and it's the best I can do without going to the city."

"I understand," said Eliza. "My mother has been known to do the very same thing."

Grandmother nodded in appreciation. "Thank you for helping Desiree, Eliza. I am most grateful."

DJ was actually relieved to get away from the house. "Whew," she said as Eliza drove them the short distance to town. "I'm glad to get out of there."

"Me too," admitted Eliza. "I heard Taylor yelling at Rhiannon in their room."

"Poor Rhiannon."

"That's for sure. Rhiannon may think she's a strong Christian, but I have a feeling that Taylor is going to be putting her to the test."

The way Eliza used the term *strong Christian* made DJ wonder if she knew more about this than she'd let on. "What did you think about what Rhiannon said last night?" asked DJ as Eliza parked in front of the Chic Boutique.

"What do you mean?"

"I mean about going to church and being a Christian."

"Well, I grew up in the Bible belt," said Eliza as they got out of the car.

"What's a Bible belt?" DJ imagined someone with a black book belted around their midsection.

"I mean there's a church on every corner down south. And although my parents didn't go to church every Sunday, not like my grandparents did, they did take us for holidays and baptisms and things like that. So I'm kind of familiar with the whole church thing."

"Does that mean you're a Christian too?" asked DJ.

"Of course."

"Oh." Now this didn't exactly compute. Or maybe there were different sorts of Christians. Or maybe things to do with religion and church were simply meant to be confusing. DJ's mother had been friends with a Christian woman named Diane before she died. They'd had some long conversations that DJ had overheard bits and pieces of, but it had made no sense to her then. And it still didn't now. Perhaps it was better not to think about these things at all. DJ followed Eliza into the salon where a petite brunette was sitting at the reception desk. Eliza told her of the appointment, and DJ looked around the shop where everything seemed to be done in shades of purples, plums, and pinks. Not exactly DJ's favorite colors.

"Oh, there you are," said a heavyset man with black curly hair and a goatee. He reached for both of Eliza's hands and looked into her face. "You must be Katherine's granddaughter Desiree. You are a beauty just like your grandmother. And I am Val."

"Actually, I'm Eliza Wilton," she told him. "But thank you!" Then she turned to where DJ was still lurking in the shadows behind her. "*This* is Mrs. Carter's granddaughter."

"Oh, I am so sorry," said Val. Then he smiled at DJ. "But you are beautiful too, Desiree. Two beautiful girls to grace my shop."

"Thank you," said DJ with embarrassment. "But you can call me DJ. I don't really go by Desiree."

He frowned. "Of course you must go by Desiree. Don't you know what it means?"

DJ nodded. "Yes. I know."

He winked at her. "Desired one. Now, what is so wrong with that?"

She shrugged. "It just doesn't seem to fit."

"Ah, but you will grow into it." He led her back into the shop now. "I think you are already growing into it."

DJ tossed Eliza a glance that was meant to convey, "Do not leave me with this lunatic," and Eliza asked if it was okay to watch.

"Certainly," said Val. "The more the merrier."

"And if I like what you do for DJ, I'll make an appointment for myself. I think I'll be ready for some touchups in about three weeks."

"That's what I like to hear." Val put a plum-colored hair-cutting shawl around DJ's shoulders then began feeling the texture of her hair. "Ah, very nice . . . and Katherine told me exactly what to do. It will be perfect."

Eliza picked up a *Vogue* and sat in the chair next to DJ. DJ attempted to relax as Val began his work. *Really*, she assured herself, *how bad could this be?* She'd liked what Eliza had done yesterday. This would simply be a more permanent version of that.

But when he was done and turned her around to see in the mirror, she was shocked. "What did you do?" she asked, as she felt her hair, unsure that it really belonged to her.

"Is something wrong?" asked Val, looking wounded.

"It's so—so blonde!" she declared.

He seemed to study her. "The highlighting took a little better than I expected. But isn't it beautiful!"

Eliza stood behind her now, nodding eagerly. "It's gorgeous, DJ."

"But it's so blonde!"

"You look fantastic," said Eliza. "Really, you do."

Now DJ looked at Eliza's reflection, just behind her. And she realized that their hair looked almost exactly alike. She swallowed against the lump in her throat, feeling tears burning behind her eyes. She did not want to be a baby. She would not cry in front of Val and Eliza. "It looks like your hair," she said to Eliza.

Eliza just seemed to notice this. "Well, it's similar. But I think your hair actually has more color and contrast to it." She lifted a strand of DJ's hair as if to prove this. "See, you can still see the brown shades underneath."

The receptionist came over now. "Oh, it's beautiful, Val," she gushed. "Maybe we should take a photo for our collection."

"Good thinking," said Val.

"Wait," said Eliza. "First let's touch up her makeup." She grabbed her bag. "Is that okay, DJ?"

DJ just shrugged. The sooner this all ended, the happier she'd be. So she sat there as Eliza applied some lip color and blush and things. Eventually the receptionist snapped a Polaroid, and when DJ saw it, she thought the girl looked like a stranger ... or perhaps a clone of Eliza.

"Very pretty," said the receptionist as she pinned the photo up with some others. "A great addition to our wall of fame."

DJ wanted to say, "Don't you mean wall of shame?" but she controlled herself and thanked them both instead.

"Are you really unhappy with it?" asked Eliza once they were outside.

"I'm in shock," admitted DJ. "I just didn't expect it to be so blonde."

"I think you'll get used to it," said Eliza as they got into the car. "Let the wind blow through your hair, tangle it a little so that the darker color shows up, and maybe you'll be happier then."

"Maybe ..." Still DJ was not convinced.

"And we'll get some lunch," said Eliza. "My mother says you should never make a judgment about your hair on an empty stomach."

"Right."

Just then the car next to them honked, and they both turned to see a car full of guys waiting at the stoplight next to them. The guys were smiling and waving and obviously flirting.

"See," said Eliza as she looked back toward the traffic light. "Already you're getting approval."

DJ sighed. "I just wanted to look like me."

"You do," said Eliza. "Just better."

After lunch, where Eliza grazed lightly on a bowl of vegetable soup and green salad but DJ made up for it by putting away a cheeseburger and fries, they went shopping. And Eliza could shop! For a girl who was subsiding on mostly vegetables, Eliza seemed to be fairly energetic. They hit several small shops that Eliza thought looked promising, and Eliza tirelessly perused through rack after rack, loading DJ down with things that she would then have to try on. In some ways, it seemed that Eliza was wearing DJ down. And before long, DJ wasn't even sure what she did or didn't like. Instead, she surrendered herself to Eliza's taste and her grandmother's finances. She just wanted to get this over with and go where she promised herself she would take a nice long nap.

By the time they got to Macy's, which Eliza seemed to feel might be their best bet, DJ already had numerous bags. And all the cash her grandmother had given her was spent. In Macy's, Eliza managed to find even more items that she was absolutely convinced "DJ could not live without." This added up to more times in the dressing rooms, more standing in front of the dreadful three-way mirrors and bad lighting, while Eliza determined whether a certain shirt, blouse, skirt, or pair of pants was acceptable or not.

Ironically, the more times DJ saw herself in these unforgiving mirrors, the more she got used to her new hair. Sure, it didn't look like her. Not the old her. But it wasn't unattractive either. And it hadn't escaped her notice that people, including salesclerks, waitresses, and even strangers, were treating her differently. At first she thought it was only because she was with pretty Eliza, but then she realized that wasn't the only factor.

Still, as Eliza drove them home with the car piled high with bags, mostly belonging to DJ, it bothered her that she had caved—both to Eliza and her grandmother. And it stunned her to realize that only two days ago she had still been DJ the tomboy, wearing a ball cap, unflattering jeans, grubby flip-flops, and T-shirts. And yet she'd been perfectly happy in that old uniform. Hadn't she?

"I'm exhausted," said DJ as Eliza parked her car by the house. "I'm taking a nap before we go out tonight."

"Harry said they'll be by around six-thirty," said Eliza as she helped DJ carry the packages inside. "They're taking us to dinner first, then the movie."

DJ turned and looked at Eliza as they paused on the porch to open the door. "What if Conner doesn't like my hair?"

Eliza frowned. "Why wouldn't he?"

"He told me he liked me the way I was. He said he didn't like high-maintenance girls."

160

Eliza just laughed. "I would hardly describe you as high maintenance, DJ. And you look beautiful. What guy in his right mind wouldn't appreciate that?"

DJ just shrugged as they went inside. "I don't know ..."

"Don't worry so much," said Eliza as they went up the stairs. "You'll give yourself frown lines."

Then, as DJ stood in front of her bedroom door, she felt a wave of apprehension. She did not want to take all these new clothes into her bedroom and face Casey now. She could just imagine the grief that Casey was going to give her.

"What's wrong?" asked Eliza as DJ stood frozen in front of her closed door.

"I—uh—"

"Here, let me help," offered Eliza, reaching past her to open the door. Then Eliza walked in and dumped the bags onto DJ's bed.

"What is going on?" demanded Casey, still sitting exactly where she'd been when DJ had left that morning. Had she been there all day? Playing that horrible computer game?

"Nothing," said Eliza as she heaped even more bags onto her bed.

"What is all that?"

"See y'all later," called Eliza pleasantly as she closed the door.

"And what happened to your hair?" Casey set her laptop aside and came over to stare at DJ.

"I got it highlighted," said DJ as she went over to see herself in the mirror. Oddly enough, she was sort of starting to like it now. Eliza had been right, having it tousled by the wind seemed to help. The darker hair showed up more now and it was actually sort of interesting, although different.

"You look just like Eliza," said Casey, as if that were a

161

horrible thing. "You guys are like a couple of Barbie dolls. Maybe we should call you Barbie One and Barbie Two. Or, better yet, Eliza can be Kentucky Barbie and you can be California Barbie. Or maybe she can be Barbie Belle and you can—"

"Knock it off," snapped DJ.

Casey blinked. Then sighing loudly, she returned to the window seat and her laptop.

"Sorry," said DJ. "But I didn't appreciate—"

"Forget about it." Now the game was making its shooting and screaming noises again.

"Would you mind turning that down?" asked DJ, trying to use a nicer tone of voice. She really didn't want to fight with Casey.

"Yeah, whatever."

Then DJ moved the bags from her bed, piling them on the floor next to it, flopped down and closed her eyes. She felt so many different emotions just now. On one hand, she was looking forward to going out with Conner. And yet she was worried about how he'd react to her hair. She remembered complaining to him about how shallow the Carter House girls all were. And now it seemed as if she were becoming one of them. Even Casey could see it. Still, maybe it was part of growing up. Maybe it was about time for DJ to pay more attention to her previously neglected appearance.

DJ thought about her mother now, remembering how she'd often said that it was more important for DJ to be herself than to fit into other people's expectations for her. Her mom had encouraged her to do sports. Whether it was swimming, soccer, basketball, volleyball, or karate, Mom had supported her in it. And she had come to as many games and meets as she could, sometimes sneaking out of her real estate office just to be DJ's biggest fan.

Mom had never minded that DJ wanted to be a tomboy. She had never forced DJ to wear frilly dresses or "act like a lady." She had let DJ simply be what she wanted to be. Even when DJ's dad discouraged this, Mom had stayed firm. In fact, DJ had blamed herself when their marriage began to deteriorate. She thought if she hadn't been such a tomboy, maybe her dad would stick around. But her mom and a year of meeting with a counselor convinced her otherwise. Her dad had left simply because he wanted to go. DJ found out, after Mom died, that he'd been involved with Jan while he was still married. Maybe it was then that she dug in her heels and determined that she would always be a tomboy . . . just to spite him.

DJ had begun to understand, after living with her grandmother these past several months, that her mom's attitude about DJ might have been related to how she'd been raised. Growing up in Manhattan, attending private schools, having a famous fashion-minded mother who expected perfection from everyone, and finally being groomed for a career in fashion, which she eventually rejected, DJ's mother had good reason to want something different for her own daughter. It was no wonder that she'd allowed and encouraged DJ to be whatever she wanted to be.

But now, more than ever, DJ felt as if she had compromised all that. In just two quick days, DJ had turned into the very thing that she had despised. How was that even possible? And why was growing up so hard?

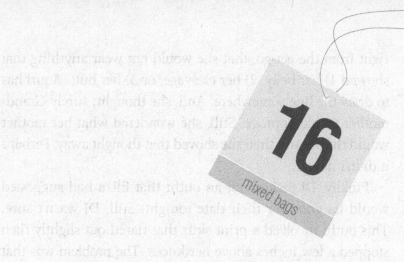

16

mixed bags

When DJ woke, Casey was gone, although her abandoned laptop was still on the window seat. It was a little past five, and DJ thought this might be her chance to get ready for her date—her first real date—without an audience. Because the last thing DJ needed right now was Casey's disapproval. The truth was DJ had enough disapproval of her own making. But as she showered and messed with her hair and then put on a little bit of the makeup that Eliza had coerced her into buying today, she tried to push away her conflicted thoughts. She told herself that she was cooperating in this major makeover because it was what she really wanted deep down. And that was partially true—she did want to look pretty. She just hoped it wasn't a big mistake.

Still in her bathrobe, she began to hang up the items she'd purchased that day. As she removed price tags and examined them a bit more closely, holding them up in the mirror to see, she decided that Eliza actually had done a pretty good job as a shopping advisor. Although the clothes were a whole lot more fashionable than what DJ had been used to, there was still a sensible quality to them. DJ had made it clear to Eliza, right from the get-go, that she would not wear anything that showed 1) her belly, 2) her cleavage, or 3) her butt. A girl has to draw the line somewhere. And, she thought, surely Grandmother would approve. Still, she wondered what her mother would think. And then she shoved that thought away. Perhaps it didn't matter.

Finally, DJ picked out an outfit that Eliza had suggested would be good for their date tonight. Still, DJ wasn't sure. This outfit involved a print skirt that flared out slightly then stopped a few inches above her knees. The problem was that DJ hadn't worn a skirt in ... well, like, forever. Still, she decided to try it on. And she had to admit that it didn't look half bad. And it did have a nice feeling when she moved around the room, kind of swishing around her legs. Next she put on the top combination that Eliza had liked with this skirt. It began with a lace-trimmed, coffee-colored camisole that was topped in a silky shirt in a soft mossy shade of green that Eliza had said looked classy and brought out the green in DJ's eyes. And it did look nice with the skirt. And feminine too. All in all, she thought she actually looked pretty good. Still, she wasn't sure what shoes to wear. Maybe she'd ask Eliza about that.

"Well, now," said Casey as she came into the room. "Don't you look nice. What's the special occasion? Oh, let me guess ... a date?"

DJ looked evenly at Casey now. She felt like she'd had enough. If she and Casey were going to share this room for a whole year, they might as well deal with this ... this ... whatever it was. "Okay, Casey, let's get whatever is eating you out in the open. Why do you have it out for me? What have I done to deserve being treated like this?"

Casey just shrugged and then slumped back down onto the window seat.

"Come on, Casey. We used to be friends. We used to tell each other everything."

"Well, you've changed."

"*I've* changed?" DJ could hear the shrillness in her voice now. "Have you seen yourself lately, Casey?" Then she reached down, grabbed Casey's hand and pulled her up so the two of them could stand in front of the mirror. "What about *you?*"

"Fine. We've both changed," admitted Casey as she frowned at their reflection.

"Right. And people change." DJ stared at Casey now. She looked so totally different from DJ. So dark and somber in her dark clothing and clumpy boots, even though it was summer. Not to mention she was slightly scary with those safety pins through her eyebrows.

"I liked you better before," said Casey.

"Ditto back at you." DJ held her chin higher now.

"But you're becoming just like the others," said Casey. "Like a Stepford teen." She pointed at the skirt. "Look at you, you used to hate dresses."

"Look at you," said DJ, pointing to a safety pin. "You used to cry if you accidentally got poked by a rosebush thorn."

Casey almost smiled now. "Yeah, well, you're right. People change."

"Why?" asked DJ.

"I don't know."

"I think you do."

"It's a long story." Casey turned away from the mirror. "And you have a date tonight."

"Not for a—"

"And I need to use the bathroom." Then Casey clumped off into the bathroom, firmly closing the door as if to signify the end of the conversation. And maybe that was just as well since it was a little past six now. DJ went over to Eliza's room and knocked on the door. Kriti answered then smiled. "Don't you look pretty."

"Thanks," said DJ. "Is Eliza around?"

"In here," called Eliza from the bathroom. "Just doing some last-minute primping." She emerged and clapped her hands. "Look at you!"

DJ did a little spin, then felt embarrassed for doing it. "But I don't know what shoes to wear."

Eliza studied DJ for a moment. "I have just the thing." Then she scurried off to her closet and returned with a pretty pair of sandals, the same shade of brown as her camisole. "And you need some jewelry. Are your ears pierced?"

"No way," said DJ as she remembered the safety pins in her roommate's eyebrows.

Eliza laughed. "Well, then the necklace will have to do." She came around from behind DJ and fastened a necklace. "Go and check it out."

DJ stood in front of their mirror and smiled. "That's nice."

"You look great," said Kriti.

"Thanks," said DJ. "It's totally different from what I'm used to."

"We're aware of that," teased Eliza.

"But it feels pretty good."

"Cool." Eliza turned away. "Now, I better finish up. You're going to be some serious competition tonight, girlfriend."

DJ wanted to say that she didn't want to compete with anyone when it came to looks, but it was too late — Eliza had closed the door behind her.

"Tell Eliza I'll meet her downstairs, okay?"

"Sure." Kriti held up the book she'd been reading last night. "I'm halfway done now."

"Wow, you're fast."

"It's a compelling book," said Kriti. "And a good way to learn some American history."

Just as DJ was going downstairs, she heard the dinner bell ring. Fortunately, they'd already informed Grandmother of their plans. But DJ was curious as to how her grandmother would react to this outfit. For that reason, she decided to make an appearance in the dining room.

"Oh, Desiree," gushed her grandmother. "You look very pretty." She came closer to examine her hair. "Val did a good job."

"It was lighter than I wanted."

"I think it's perfect." Grandmother stepped back as if to study her. "But stand up straight, dear."

DJ complied.

"Better."

"And you remember that Eliza and I are going out tonight?"

"Oh, yes, I forgot to tell Clara two fewer places. Oh well."

The girls were starting to come in for dinner now. Taylor eyed DJ with hostile suspicion, but said nothing. Probably because Grandmother was in the room. Rhiannon gave DJ a smile and a thumbs-up. DJ wanted to ask how she was faring with her cranky roommate. Too bad she and Rhiannon couldn't swap. Then again, DJ wasn't sure she wanted to hear that much about Rhiannon's religious beliefs. As difficult as Casey was being, at least she didn't preach at her. Not that Rhiannon preached exactly. But sometimes the things she said sounded a little too high and mighty, a little too good to be true.

Then Eliza came to get DJ, saying that the guys were already there. They told the others good-bye and then, feeling

169

like quite the socialite, DJ followed Eliza out to the foyer where Harry and Conner were waiting.

"Don't you girls look gorgeous," said Harry.

Conner seemed slightly surprised when he saw DJ, but then smiled. "You changed your hair."

DJ nodded. Then as they went outside, she explained that between her grandmother, Eliza, and the hairdresser, she hadn't really had much choice. Yet even as she said this, she thought it sounded pretty lame. Like she had suddenly turned into the victim. And that irritated her.

"It looks good," he said, and she thanked him.

"You girls okay to ride in the Jeep?" asked Harry. "Or would you rather take your car?"

Eliza considered this then reached in her bag and handed over her keys to Harry. "My car. We want to be treated like ladies tonight."

He grinned. "No problem."

DJ felt a little uneasy getting into the backseat with Conner. For some reason it seemed to drive home the fact that this was a date. A real date. And her first one. Not that she planned to let that cat out of the bag.

DJ was surprised to find out that Harry had made reservations at South Port, the fanciest restaurant in town. He explained that he'd had his dad do it for him, since the restaurant owner was a friend. "And being that it's Saturday and Labor Day weekend, they were booked. Or so they told me when I tried to get a table. But then my dad stepped in, and it was like no problem."

DJ felt completely out of her element as they were seated at a white cloth-covered table next to the window that overlooked the bay. But then she looked across to where Eliza appeared totally relaxed. And that's when DJ decided that she would simply imitate Eliza. When Eliza put her linen napkin in her lap, DJ followed suit. When Eliza opened the big menu, DJ did as well. She tried to be inconspicuous about it, but it got so bad that when Eliza wiped her mouth with her napkin midway through the meal, DJ did the same.

Finally, the meal was over. Eliza thanked Harry for dinner, and DJ did likewise with Conner. But as she did this, she noticed something in Conner's expression that worried her. He seemed a little less interested in her than he had been the day before.

"Want to walk down the docks?" asked Conner. "We have about twenty minutes before the movie starts." They all agreed, but no sooner were they on the wooden docks when DJ realized that she had a problem. The sandals that Eliza had loaned her had spike heels that kept getting caught between the boards. Eventually DJ was walking like a penguin just to keep from falling on her face. Eliza was lucky to be wearing platform sandals, and she was walking just fine. She and Harry were almost to the end of the dock by now.

"Maybe we should go back," suggested Conner.

"Yeah," agreed DJ. "Maybe so." She considered simply removing the sandals and going barefoot. But the idea of putting her dirty feet back into the borrowed shoes seemed wrong. So she toughed it out.

Back on solid land, Conner leaned his head back, looked up at the sky, and let out a big breath.

"Everything okay?" she asked.

"Huh?" He turned and looked at her. "Oh, yeah. I was just thinking about school starting in three days ... and soccer and stuff."

"Oh."

And then they just stood there without talking until Harry

and Eliza came back. "We saw the funniest boat," Eliza told them. "It was like a combination of a submarine and a boat, like something that someone had put together himself."

"It looked like something out of a bad James Bond movie," said Harry. "You guys should go see it."

"Maybe later," said Conner, glancing at his watch. "If we want to catch the beginning of the movie, we should go."

The movie was okay ... or maybe just so-so. But it was a relief to be able to just sit without talking. DJ was feeling more and more uncomfortable with this whole dating thing. She wondered why everyone acted like it was so cool. Even her dinner was starting to feel like a lump of hard clay in the pit of her stomach. More than ever she wished she'd been like Kriti, home with a good book.

After the movie, they went outside and walked the couple of blocks back to the car.

"What a gorgeous night," said Eliza happily. Then she pointed toward the bay. "And look, there's supposed to be a full moon tonight. I think I can see the light beginning to appear." She grabbed Harry by the hand and began hurrying to the car. "Let's go someplace where we can watch it come up over the water."

So they hopped into the car, and Harry drove a few minutes away where he parked in a wide-open space that faced the bay, and they sat there and watched as the round white moon cut a bright white stripe through the water.

"Isn't it beautiful," gushed Eliza.

"Not as beautiful as you," said Harry as he reached over and pulled her face toward him. Then, right in front of Conner and DJ, they began to kiss. And for some reason this just made DJ mad. If those two wanted to clean each other's teeth, it seemed like they could've taken a little stroll and done it privately. She was tempted to say something, but it was just so awkward. She wanted to look at Conner and see how he was reacting, but she was worried that he might think she was hinting for him to do the same thing. And, at the moment, she was not interested. Not that she didn't want Conner to kiss her again. She definitely did. But not like this. Not like they were simply imitating the moonstruck lovers in the front seat.

DJ folded her arms across her front and leaned back in the seat. If this car had back doors, she would most certainly have gotten out and marched away, hoping that Conner would follow. As it was, without making a complete spectacle of herself by hopping over the side of the convertible, she would have to endure this.

"Hey, maybe you guys should get a room," said Conner finally.

Harry and Eliza slowly peeled themselves apart. "Sorry," breathed Harry. "Guess the moon got to me."

Eliza giggled. "Me too."

"Want to take a moonlight stroll?" asked Harry eagerly.

"Certainly," said Eliza. "That way we can give DJ and Conner some privacy."

And before anyone could say anything, Harry and Eliza were out of the car and taking off down a trail.

"Well, that's a relief," said DJ, loosening her arms from her front and relaxing a little. "I'm not really into watching couples making out."

"Me neither."

Then they sat there in silence for a while. Finally Conner slipped his arm around her shoulders and pulled her closer to him. He looked down at her with a curious expression. "You've changed, DJ."

She tried not to feel exasperated. "So I've heard."

Then without saying another word, he kissed her. Then he kissed her again. And she kissed him back, and before long they were going at it just as vigorously as Harry and Eliza had been. And for a brief blurry moment, DJ wondered if she was still imitating her friend. Then she blocked that thought out and simply got lost in the arms and kisses of Conner. She felt her heart racing and all sorts of amazing sensations that she had never felt before. And, although it was a little scary to feel like this, it was exciting too. And, although she wanted him to stop, so she could come up for air and gather her wits, she wanted him to just keep going too.

Finally, as if in a dream, she pushed him away from her and tried to catch her breath. "That's enough," she gasped. Harry and Eliza were coming back now, holding hands and singing a silly song. DJ pushed her rumpled clothes back into place as they got into the car.

"Looks like someone enjoyed their privacy," said Eliza, turning to smile at them.

Conner sat up straighter, acting as if nothing whatsoever had just happened. And DJ was asking herself, what really had just happened? Everything had moved so quickly. One moment he was passionately kissing her, and then his hands were wandering all over her. And she hadn't even stopped him.

"Well, if we're going to make curfew, we better head home," said Eliza.

"When's curfew?" asked Harry.

"Eleven on weekends," said Eliza. "Unless we have permission to stay out later."

"Do you?" asked Harry hopefully.

"Not tonight."

So Harry drove Eliza's car home, and the boys walked

them up to the porch were "proper" good-night kisses were exchanged, and then they went their separate ways.

"Wow, you guys were really getting into it in the backseat," whispered Eliza after the front door was closed.

DJ glanced around the dimly let foyer, curious as to whether anyone was around to overhear, but all was quiet and most of the lights were off. It seemed everyone had gone to bed. Still, she didn't say anything.

"You didn't actually do it, did you?"

DJ looked at Eliza with a shocked expression. "You mean it, as in have sex?" she whispered.

Eliza giggled and nodded.

"No way."

"Oh, that's a relief."

"How about you?" asked DJ with concern as she remembered the condoms in the Hermès bag that Eliza had given her. The same bag she was using tonight. Perhaps those really were Eliza's.

"Are you kidding? On a first date? *Never.*"

DJ felt slightly relieved. But she still wondered what that meant. Did Eliza do it on a second date? Third? What were the rules about such things anyway? And who should DJ ask? Then, just as they started up the stairs, DJ heard a creak and noticed that library door was moving slightly. Perhaps it was just the shifting of old house, or perhaps something more. Whatever it was, DJ felt too drained to figure it out just now.

17

mixed bags

"Excuse me," said Mrs. Carter to the girls around the table as she set down her coffee cup with a clink. They were just finishing breakfast and DJ had noticed that her grandmother had been unusually quiet this morning.

"Desiree," said Grandmother in a stern tone as she stood. "Come to my office, please."

"Does anyone want to go to church with me?" offered Rhiannon as the others began to excuse themselves from the table. But the girls just said "no thanks" or made jokes.

As DJ left the dining room, she felt sorry for Rhiannon who was doing her best to befriend these girls. But at the same time, DJ didn't want to go either. Not that she particularly wanted to go to her grandmother's office. DJ had a feeling she'd done something wrong and was about to get into trouble, although she couldn't remember doing anything too serious. As she followed her into her office, she wondered if perhaps church might be better than a lecture from her grandmother.

Grandmother closed the door to the office now. Not a good sign. "Please, sit down, *young lady*." Using the term *young lady* was an even worse sign. Her grandmother definitely sounded irritated.

"What's wrong?" asked DJ as she sat in the chair across from her grandmother.

Now Grandmother frowned so deeply that DJ was convinced that the Botox injections must've completely worn off. "I have been informed that you did not behave yourself in a respectable manner while on your date last night, Desiree."

DJ was stunned. "What? How did you hear something like that?"

"Let us just say that a little bird told me."

DJ remembered how Eliza and Harry had discovered her and Conner in a slightly compromising position—not that they'd actually done anything seriously wrong. Still, DJ wasn't proud of herself. But, surely, Eliza wouldn't report this to her grandmother. And if she had, DJ could easily accuse Eliza and Harry of as much and possibly more.

"What exactly did this little bird say?" asked DJ in a controlled voice.

Grandmother cleared her throat. "She said that she was worried that you might be engaging in ... how do I put this delicately?"

"Why don't you just spit it out?"

"She said she was concerned that you might be having unprotected sex."

DJ blinked then stared at her grandmother. "Who said that?"

"Never mind about who said it, Desiree. The concern is whether or not you are behaving respectably and responsibly."

"What does that mean?"

"It means that I do not want my granddaughter or any of

the other Carter House girls to go about town having casual sex with their boyfriends. Nor do I want them to have unprotected sex."

"What are you saying?" demanded DJ. "Are you saying that it's okay to have sex as long as I do it in a respectable way? Like maybe get a hotel room and light candles and wear a —"

"That is not what I mean." Grandmother narrowed her eyes. "I am only saying that I expect you to act like a lady, Desiree. And if you choose to engage in sexual activities, I expect you to be responsible and mature about it."

"So, you don't care if I have sex?"

"It is not my decision whether you have sex or not. I only ask that you not embarrass me or the other girls."

DJ felt like screaming just now. "Okay, in the first place I have never had sex. Not last night. Not ever. In the second place, whoever told you this is totally lying."

"I didn't expect you to admit to anything, Desiree. I'm only trying to make it perfectly clear what my expectations are."

"You mean that I don't embarrass you?"

"Or yourself."

"And that's what matters most?"

"You may not appreciate this now, but someday you will understand that a woman's reputation can make or break her."

"So, you're saying it's fine to sleep around, just don't get caught ... and don't get a sexually transmitted disease?"

Grandmother pressed her lips together as she gave DJ a very disgusted and disappointed look. As if answering that question was far below her dignity.

"I'm just trying to get some clarity, Grandmother." DJ stood now.

"It's not easy taking on six girls," said Grandmother.

"It makes it even harder when my own granddaughter misbehaves."

"I did *not* misbehave," said DJ, although she wasn't completely sure this was true. Mostly she felt confused.

"When I receive a complaint from one of the girls, I must take it seriously, Desiree."

"Even if it's untrue?"

"How will I know that it's untrue until I investigate?"

"And what if the complaint comes from me? Would you investigate that?"

Grandmother looked somewhat uncertain now.

"Or perhaps my opinions and concerns don't matter here."

"What I'm trying to say is that I expect more from you, Desiree."

"How fair is that?"

"Life is not fair, Desiree. The sooner you figure that out, the smarter you will be."

"I think I already know that." DJ frowned. "Is that all?"

"I believe I have made myself clear."

"Crystal." In fact, DJ felt she could see right through the old woman just now. All her grandmother cared about was looking good—that the Carter House girls looked good, and that DJ looked good and didn't embarrass anyone. That was perfectly clear. As DJ left the office, she noticed Taylor going up the stairs. Of course, Taylor had to be the "little bird." Who else would do something like that? Taylor was probably responsible for the creaking door last night. She must've been hiding in the shadows and eavesdropping when Eliza initiated the stupid sex conversation. And, naturally, it was Taylor who went whining to Grandmother this morning. It all made sense.

The question was, what should DJ do about it? Or perhaps she should do nothing. Maybe she should pretend that everything was perfectly fine. After all, it wasn't as if DJ was being punished for something. Sure, it stung to be falsely accused and lectured like that, but then DJ knew her grandmother had on blinders when it came to girls who came from impressive or wealthy families. Girls like Taylor or Eliza, or even Kriti. DJ knew she should get used to favoritism in Carter House. Being a relative would not protect her from anything.

Casey hadn't come down for breakfast this morning. DJ had tried to wake her, but Casey had simply growled and turned over. Still, DJ felt sorry for her. In some ways, she knew how Casey felt. Even so, she thought that Casey was going about everything in a very negative way—a way that would probably hurt Casey more than it would hurt anyone else. DJ decided to get something from the kitchen to take up to her.

"What are you doing in here?" demanded Clara when she caught DJ poking around in the oversized refrigerator.

"I'm getting Casey some breakfast."

"If Casey is hungry, she should show up when it's time to eat," snapped Clara.

"Look, she's having kind of a hard time," said DJ. "It's not going to make things better to starve her."

Clara softened a bit now. "You're probably right. There are some yogurts in the back there; she might like one of those."

DJ thanked Clara, and then took an apple, a yogurt, and a muffin up to Casey, who was just getting up.

"Good morning," said DJ as she set her bounty on Casey's bedside table. "Thought you might be hungry since you missed breakfast."

"Thanks," said Casey as she ran her hands through her

181

wild-looking hair. She still had on the same clothes she'd been wearing yesterday.

DJ sat down on the window seat now. "I just got lectured by my grandmother."

Casey looked up with interest. "Why?"

"Someone told her that I'd been having unprotected sex."

Casey looked surprised. "Have you?"

DJ shook her head. "No, of course not."

"Have you been having *any* kind of sex?"

"No. Not at all."

Casey looked relieved.

"I'm pretty sure it was Taylor who told her that," said DJ.

Casey picked up the apple and took a big bite. "I hate Taylor."

"She's a real piece of work," said DJ.

"I thought I was going to slug her last night when she came at me," said Casey. "She was asking for it."

"Have you ever been in a real fight?" asked DJ. "I mean like hitting and kicking and stuff." DJ remembered seeing a girl fight at her old high school. It had been sort of fascinating, but sickening at the same time.

"I've been beat up."

"Really?"

Casey nodded as she opened the yogurt.

"Why?"

"Because I didn't fit in."

"Oh ..." DJ diverted her stare away from Casey's strange hair and pierced eyebrows.

"I know what you're thinking," said Casey. "You think I didn't fit in because I look like this. But the truth is I looked totally normal when I got beat up. I didn't fit in because I was

182

trying to act like a nice Christian. I was trying to be a good little girl."

DJ didn't know what to say. "You got beat up for that?"

"Most of my algebra class had been caught cheating on a final. I was one of the few who didn't cheat, and when the guidance counselor asked me some questions about what had happened, I told her the truth."

"So you got beat up for telling the truth?"

"Everyone assumed that I'd given names, but I hadn't. Some girls in that class were really ticked, and they started to take their aggressions out on me when no one was looking."

"Why didn't you tell?"

"I did. Things just got worse." Casey scowled. "My parents kept saying things like 'turn the other cheek' or to 'love my enemies.' Sometimes they even insinuated that I was part of the problem. Eventually I got fed up."

"That would be tough."

"So, I decided to change. I was tired of being picked on, especially for something I wasn't really into. I mean I only went to church and stuff because my parents made me. It wasn't my choice."

"So that's when you started to dress differently?"

"Yep." Casey took a bite of muffin and crumbs spilled all over her bed, but she just let them.

"Didn't your parents care?"

"Of course, they cared. Man, we had some wild fights. Then I would sneak clothes out of the house and change when I got to school. Finally, my mom talked to a friend who told her to lighten up on me. They thought if they acted like they didn't care, I would quit dressing like this."

"But that didn't work."

"Nope. I pushed things even harder. It was kind of fun

watching them acting like it was no big deal. It's like you could see them actually biting their tongues. Then I'd hear them discussing me behind closed doors. They even got into fights about it." She frowned. "I did feel kinda bad about that."

"But not bad enough to go back to normal."

"I was sick of normal. And when I started dressing like this, I began to make a completely different set of friends. And the girls who had been bullying me quit. Oh, they'd still say mean things, but no one picked a fight with me. I think they were scared."

DJ could imagine that. Even though she'd known Casey for years and had been good friends with her, she found her appearance a little frightening now. "But do you like looking like that?" she asked.

Casey just shrugged.

"Does it make you feel good?"

"I've given up on feeling good."

"Why?"

"Because it's a crock." Casey pointed at DJ now. "Does the way you look make you feel good?"

DJ considered this. "I don't know ..."

"Because I think you've compromised yourself. I think you're becoming like Eliza and the others just to fit in. And that's a sellout."

Just then someone knocked on the door, and DJ was relieved to jump up and get it. "Hey, Eliza," said DJ. "Wanna come in?"

"No. I was just going to town. I noticed there was a Starbucks there yesterday. I thought I'd get a mocha. Do you want to join me?"

"Sure," said DJ eagerly. She turned to Casey now. "Do you want to come too?"

"To Starbucks?" Casey looked as if they'd just invited her to go to the local sewage-treatment plant. "I don't think so."

DJ wanted to ask her why, but figured that might only open up a new can of worms. Instead she just grabbed her bag and told Casey she'd see her later. Mostly she was glad to escape from her. Casey was not a happy camper.

"I thought we'd walk," said Eliza when they were outside. "I need some exercise."

"Sounds great," said DJ. "I usually walk to town."

"So what was up with Mrs. Carter this morning? She sounded a little irate."

DJ gave her the lowdown, and Eliza agreed that it was probably Taylor's doing. "We should think of a way to shut that girl down before she does some real damage."

DJ nodded. "She's definitely out to get me."

"She's a loose cannon, DJ. I think she's out to get anybody who doesn't bow down and worship her."

"Well, if you have any brilliant ideas for stopping her, I'm in," said DJ as they went into Starbucks.

Eliza ordered a sugar-free, nonfat mocha, and although DJ wondered what the point was, she did likewise. Then they sat down and talked about last night's date and whether or not Harry and Conner were serious about them. Eliza was just assuring DJ that she thought Conner was smitten by her when Eliza's cell phone rang. DJ could tell that it was Harry, and then Eliza said, "We'd love to come. It sounds like fun." Then she hung up.

"What?" asked DJ curiously.

"Harry is having a party at his beach house tomorrow."

"I thought he said someone was using it over Labor Day weekend."

"Sounds like they're leaving in the morning. He's inviting

a bunch of friends from school. He wants us to meet everyone before school starts on Tuesday."

"Oh …" DJ didn't admit that she already knew some of them, or that some of them hadn't been very nice to her. Maybe that was about to change.

"I told him we'd come," said Eliza. "I hope that was okay."

"Of course," said DJ. "Can I assume Conner will be there?"

"Naturally."

"Cool." Maybe this would give DJ a chance to really talk to him. She felt like they'd sort of been hung out to dry last night, and now she wanted to make sure everything was okay between them.

"Oh, yeah, Harry said the other girls were invited too."

"All of them?" asked DJ.

Eliza laughed. "Well, we can't really exclude anyone, can we?"

"I guess not."

"Besides, it might be a way to put some of the girls—particularly Taylor—in their places."

DJ nodded like that was a good idea. But the truth was she wasn't sure that it was even possible. And what about Casey? How would she possibly fit into this crowd? Or maybe that wasn't DJ's problem.

All the Carter House girls decided to go to Harry's beach-house party. DJ had hidden her surprise when Casey agreed to go. Hopefully, this would help Casey. Maybe she would realize that it was time to change her rebel-girl image. Because there were six of them and Eliza's car was small, DJ talked her grandmother into letting her use her car as well. DJ would've preferred riding in Eliza's Porsche, but at least she wasn't stuck in the same vehicle as Taylor. Naturally, Taylor opted to ride with Eliza, taking the front seat as if she were privileged. Kriti rode in the back.

"So the royalty rides with Eliza," observed Casey as DJ pulled out into the street. "And the less fortunate with you?"

"Are you complaining?" asked DJ with a little irritation.

"Just commenting."

"I don't feel unfortunate," said Rhiannon from the backseat.

"That's because you're a freaking Pollyanna," said Casey.

"Be nice," warned DJ.

"I can't believe I agreed to come," said Casey when DJ pulled up into the crowded driveway. "This is probably a big fat mistake."

"Just make the best of it," said DJ as she turned off the ignition and grabbed her bag. DJ had dressed carefully tonight, and she'd made sure to get Eliza's stamp of approval—doing this while Casey was taking a shower so she wouldn't hear her and tease. But as DJ got out of the car, she felt confident. She could hold her own with the Crescent Cove girls.

Eliza was just getting out of her car, which was parked closer to the house. She waved at DJ and waited for her to join them. Loud music was coming from the house, and the whole place was lit up, making quite an impression against the dusky sky.

"Ready to partee?" asked Taylor, flashing an unexpected smile.

DJ just nodded. She still didn't trust this girl. But, naturally, Taylor would be wearing her party face tonight. And, of course, she was dressed impeccably. And her hair and makeup were perfect. DJ hated to admit it, but Taylor was stunning. No wonder Grandmother catered to her so much. Of all the girls, Taylor had the kind of looks that could make it on a New York runway. Plus she had that dog-eat-dog personality to go with it. And it was obvious that Taylor cared about making a good first impression tonight. She would probably be on her best behavior. At least on the surface.

Harry welcomed the girls and introduced them around. And although DJ could sense some malicious stares, coming primarily from the same girls who had been mean to her last spring, she could tell that for the most part, she was being accepted. As were Eliza and Taylor and Kriti. She wasn't too sure about Rhiannon, although when Bradford Wales showed up, that changed some.

Bradford was one of those guys who seemed to fit into all circles. He could mix with the art crowd, rub elbows with jocks, or hang with the academics. DJ's theory was this was because first, his family was very wealthy, second, his mother was a renowned artist, and third, he was good-looking in a tall, dark, slightly gangly way. Plus, he had a pleasant personality. Also, DJ noticed, he seemed genuinely drawn to Rhiannon. They hadn't exactly been dating last year, but DJ suspected that was about to change.

DJ still hadn't spotted Conner yet, but she tried not to look overly concerned as she watched Harry and Eliza dancing and mixing easily with the crowd. Those two were like the king and queen of the party, and it was plain to see that Eliza would have no problem fitting in at Crescent Cove High. She certainly didn't need DJ by her side. In fact, DJ had a strong suspicion that Eliza's friendship was something she shouldn't count on. That's when DJ noticed Casey hanging on the sidelines and looking like her recently unhappy self. DJ knew she should try to help her old friend, but how? At the moment, it felt as if DJ was barely keeping her nose above water.

Meanwhile, Taylor was still talking and joking — or was it flirting? — with Bradford Wales. And yet Rhiannon seemed perfectly comfortable with this intrusion into her relationship. She smiled and nodded as if she thought Taylor wasn't the slightest threat. Or maybe Rhiannon was that confident. But how? In many ways that girl was just a flat-out mystery to DJ.

"Want to check out the eats?" DJ suddenly asked Kriti. It was something to do and seemed preferable to standing around and waiting for Conner to show. Kriti agreed, and they headed over to where a granite-topped island was filled with the kinds of foods that were strictly forbidden in Carter House. DJ got a paper plate and began to fill it with carbs and calories.

"Look at that," said Kriti, nudging DJ with her elbow as she pointed to the kitchen where a stainless-steel keg was sitting on the counter by the fridge. "I should've known there'd be beer tonight."

DJ sighed. Yes, perhaps she should've known this too. Somehow, she hadn't really considered the possibility. "I'm sorry, Kriti," she said. "I didn't know."

"Well, at least *you* won't be drinking, right?" Kriti asked.

"Of course not." Even so, it made her uncomfortable that others would be. She remembered being stopped by the police the other day. What if that happened again tonight? Or worse, what if there was a wreck? Yet, at the same time, she felt aggravated that this whole thing worried her. She wished she could be like the others and just not care. Why was she always so torn about everything?

"I wonder how Rhiannon feels about it?" asked Kriti.

"That's a good question," admitted DJ.

"Where's Conner tonight?" asked Kriti after they took their plates and sodas over to a quiet corner and sat down.

"I don't know." DJ looked around the room again. "I thought he'd be here."

Before long a couple of guys came over and reintroduced themselves. Then they invited Kriti and DJ to dance. Kriti happily agreed, but DJ felt unsure. What about Conner?

"Come on," said Garrison as he reached for her hand. "I don't bite."

So, feeling somewhat dejected that Conner wasn't there, DJ went with him. She wasn't the greatest dancer, but thankfully the lights were low and the music was loud and lively, and she decided to just have fun with it. It made no sense to be uncertain about everything. Good grief, it was like she didn't even know her own mind.

But midway through the dance, she saw Conner arrive and her heart leaped. He seemed to spot her too, but when she

190

waved at him, he just turned away and started talking to another guy. Well, this irked her, and when Garrison asked her to dance the next one, she decided to just go with the flow. Maybe it would give Conner something to consider. Maybe it would teach him for coming late ... for not calling her once after their date.

But she felt a little concerned when the song turned out to be a slow one and she found herself dancing very close to Garrison. But the next thing she knew Conner was dancing with, of all people, Taylor! And that just made DJ plain mad. Still, she tried not to show it, and when the song ended, she thanked Garrison and went over to where Conner was now standing with Taylor.

"Hey," she said in an even voice. "You made it."

He nodded. "Yeah, I got waylaid on the home front."

"Oh ..." She didn't know what to say now, and she could feel Taylor's eyes on her, as if she was waiting for DJ to make a scene. Perhaps a scene that would humiliate DJ in front of everyone.

"Looks like you met Garrison," said Conner.

"Yeah. I was getting kind of bored. It was nice of someone to dance with me."

"Yeah, nice."

DJ wanted Conner to ask her to dance now. She was even tempted to ask him, but for some reason, maybe it was pride, she could not. Still, she wanted him to do something to make it perfectly clear to Taylor that he really did like DJ, and that they were really a couple. But he didn't. And he didn't say anything either. They just stood there. Finally Taylor began making small talk and he responded. And that aggravated DJ even more. What was wrong with him anyway? How could he passionately kiss her one night and two nights later act as if he barely knew her?

Suddenly, she felt seriously worried. Maybe he didn't really like her. Maybe she had only imagined that he liked her. Or maybe their make-out session in Eliza's backseat had been disappointing. Maybe he'd decided he just wasn't into her after that. Or maybe he realized she wasn't his type. Maybe he thought she was cheap and easy—sort of like what her grandmother had insinuated yesterday. And just like that, all her confidence seemed to evaporate. She felt more like a loser than ever. Not only that, but she felt lost. Dressed up like a Barbie doll, she had shoved her old image of being the athlete aside, and she had pushed her hurting friend away just because she didn't fit in. And now, she realized that she didn't fit in either. DJ felt cut off, alone, and totally rejected.

"Excuse me," she said, turning and walking away. She pressed her way through the crowd and went outside and stood on the deck that overlooked the ocean—the same ocean where they had experienced their first kiss. She took in several deep breaths and tried to reassure herself that everything was just fine. Perfectly fine. She told herself that at any moment, Conner would come out and join her. He would apologize and tell her that everything was okay. But he didn't. Quite some time passed, and he never came out. Finally, DJ looked back into the house to see that the party was even livelier than before, and there in the middle of the room, Conner and Taylor were dancing again. She couldn't see Conner's face just now, but Taylor looked happy. She was laughing and smiling and totally victorious.

That's when something inside DJ just cracked. Like she could almost hear it breaking. And she felt the tears coming now, but she didn't want anyone to see her like this. She knew she had to get away. And so she decided to go out to the beach. She took off her sandals and walked through the damp sand until she found a piece of driftwood. And there she sat and sobbed. As she sobbed, she was plagued with questions. Questions that had no answers and only seemed designed to torment her more.

Why was Conner treating her like this? When had everything changed between them? Or had she just been deluded that there ever was anything in the first place? What was wrong with her? Was she the hypocrite that Casey accused her of being? Had she sold out to fit in? Would she ever fit in? Would she ever be happy? And if she would never be happy, what was the point of trying? Maybe she should just walk into the ocean, swim out as far as she could possibly swim ... and just let go. End this thing. She was almost ready to stand up when she heard a girl's voice call, "Hey, you."

DJ turned around to see Rhiannon walking toward her. DJ quickly wiped the tears with her hands, trying to act normal, which seemed rather pointless. Who was she fooling anyway?

"What's wrong?" Rhiannon sat on the log next to her.

"Nothing."

"Come on, DJ, you can talk to me."

DJ wanted her to leave. "Why aren't you with Bradford?"

"He had to go home. You know it's a school night."

"Yeah, right."

"Kriti said you just disappeared. She thought it might have something to do with Taylor dancing with Conner. Want to talk about it?"

DJ figured if there was anyone she could trust, it was probably Rhiannon. Besides it didn't look like she was going away. And so she just dumped out the whole story. "I just don't get it," she said finally. "I thought he liked me."

"Would that make you happy?" asked Rhiannon.

"Sure. Why wouldn't it?"

"I mean really, truly happy," said Rhiannon. "Deep down happy."

"I don't think that's even possible."

"It is," said Rhiannon.

"Maybe for you."

"For *everyone*, DJ."

"Yeah, right."

"Here's the deal," persisted Rhiannon. "God made us with this empty space inside. We try to fill that space with all kinds of things that we think will make us happy. Like boyfriends or fancy clothes or doing exciting things. But in the end, none of that makes us happy. Sometimes those things will even make us more miserable."

"I do feel pretty miserable."

"I know. It's because you've been trying to fill that space with the wrong things."

"So, what am I supposed to fill that space with, Rhiannon?" DJ turned and looked at her face, now illuminated by the moonlight.

Rhiannon smiled, and DJ hated to admit it, but her face looked literally radiant, and *happy*. "Jesus," she said simply. "You're supposed to fill that space with the one who made you, DJ. Jesus wants to be your best friend. He wants to help you through the hard times. And he knows what you need to live your best possible life. And you'll never get there without him."

DJ actually considered this for a long moment. Still she wasn't buying. "It sounds too good to be true."

"That's exactly what I thought at first too. But I'm living proof that it is true."

"I'll admit that you do seem happy, Rhiannon, and it seems to work for you, but I don't think it'd be the same for me."

"You'll never know, DJ ... unless you give Jesus a try."

"I wouldn't even know how to do that."

"It's simple. You just invite him into your heart."

For no explainable reason, DJ was crying again. And this time the sobs seemed to emerge from a place that was dark and deep within her. There was an ache that was more painful than just feeling rejected by Conner. It was even more painful than feeling rejected by her father ... or losing her mother. It was a deep, lonely sadness that she felt would belong to her forever. And yet she knew she couldn't endure it. She knew it would eventually devour her.

Rhiannon put an arm around DJ's shoulders now. "Want me to pray with you?"

DJ just kept sobbing, but finally she nodded. "Yes," she gasped. "I—I think I do."

"Okay," said Rhiannon calmly. "If you want to invite Jesus into your heart, you just repeat what I say, or say it in your own words if you like. It doesn't really matter *how* you say it, just as long as you *mean* it."

Then Rhiannon prayed a simple prayer. And DJ echoed the words after her. First she told God that she'd blown it and that she needed him to forgive her. Then she asked Jesus to come into her heart and to make her a new person. But, even as DJ repeated these things, she wasn't entirely sure that this would work, or that it was even real. Still, she *hoped* that it was. She truly hoped that it was not just another dead end. She knew she needed something or someone to hold onto. She desperately wanted someone who was bigger and smarter—she wanted someone who really cared about her, really loved her, someone who could change things. Maybe it was God.

"Amen," said Rhiannon happily. Then she reached over and hugged DJ. "Welcome to God's family, DJ."

DJ wiped her face with her hands again. "Really?"

"Yes. Really. You are a sister in the Lord, DJ. Your life will never be the same again."

DJ took in a long, slow breath and to her surprise, she actually *felt* something changing inside her now. She wasn't even sure how to describe this feeling, not exactly like happiness, but she did have a deep sense of peace … and hope too … like everything was going to get better.

"Wow!" DJ turned to look at Rhiannon. "I actually *feel* different."

"I know." Rhiannon was beaming. "That's because Jesus is inside you. He's filling up that empty space with himself."

"Wow!" said DJ again. She stood now, taking in another deep breath, almost as if to test whether or not this was real. "This is totally amazing—really, really cool."

Rhiannon stood too. "You're a new person, DJ."

DJ nodded. "Yeah, it feels like a beginning, like life is about to get a whole lot better, like things are going to start making sense. Is that totally crazy?"

Rhiannon laughed. "Only to people who don't get it. Once you let God into your life, everything changes. Mostly you change. And, yes, things get better. But your problems don't magically disappear. Instead, you become better at dealing with them, and that's because you have Jesus with you. He will help you."

Now DJ threw her arms around Rhiannon and hugged her. "Thank you," she cried. "Thank you so much!"

"Thank God!" said Rhiannon. "It will be so great to have a sister at Carter House. I've been praying for God to send me someone. I was hoping it would be you!"

"This is going to be a good year," said DJ. And, although she had no idea where she would fit in, or if she even would, she had a feeling that it was going to be okay. Somehow things would work out. But as she walked back toward the beach house, she noticed Conner sitting out by himself on the stairs that led up to one of the decks.

"Hey," she said to Rhiannon. "You want to let the others know that we're heading out? I want a word with Conner before we go."

"Meet you at the car in a few minutes," said Rhiannon. Then, as if she understood the need for privacy, she headed up another set of stairs.

"Hey," said DJ as she cautiously approached Conner. "What's up?"

He looked surprised when he saw her. "Nothing."

"Mind if I join you?"

He just shrugged, but she sat down anyway.

"Did I do something to offend you?" she asked, thinking that it really was the other way around. He had been the one to offend her. Still, she figured this might at least get the conversation going. And, remembering the commitment she'd just made on the beach, she felt surprising hopeful. In fact, she thought perhaps God had the key to unlock this door and to help her to win Conner back.

But he didn't answer and just shrugged again, looking down and acting like a loose piece of leather on his flip-flops was the most fascinating thing on the planet. What was wrong with him?

"So, I take it you don't want to talk?" She was ready to make a break for it now. It was one thing to take some of the blame for how this was going, but Conner was acting totally uncooperative.

"I don't know what to say." Now Conner looked up at her with those clear blue eyes, and DJ could see that there was something going on behind them. Almost as if he had been hurting as badly as she. But why? Why? Why? Why?

"Just say something," she pleaded with him. "Anything! Please!"

He continued looking at her now, gazing at her as if he were seeing deep inside of her, looking at her with an expression that seemed to say he still cared. An expression that actually filled her with hope. Then he sighed and said, "You've changed, DJ."

She considered this. Did he know that she'd just given her heart to God? Was it that obvious? "Yes," she said eagerly. "I have changed! Isn't that great?"

But he just shook his head and frowned. "I liked you better before."

"Before?" She tried to wrap her head around this. "Why?"

But he was standing now. "I gotta get outta here," he said abruptly.

"But what about—"

Before she could finish her question, he leaned down and, cupping her chin in his hand, kissed her. "Bye, DJ."

And she just sat there trying to make sense of everything that had happened tonight. What had just transpired between them? And why was Conner acting so weird? Did he still like her? Or was that supposed to be a final good-bye kiss?

But, strangely enough, she didn't feel too freaked by all this. Somehow, she knew that it was going to be okay with Conner. One way or another, with God's help, things would work out. She felt certain of that.

This wasn't the end . . . no, it was the beginning.

carter house girls

stealing bradford

melody carlson
bestselling author

Read these bonus chapters of *Stealing Bradford*, Book 2 in the Carter House Girls series.

1

stealing bradford

"I'm sorry, but my car's just not big enough for *all* the girls," announced Eliza as they were finishing breakfast. She pushed a glossy strand of blonde hair away from her face and then took a slow sip of coffee. As usual, Eliza was stylishly dressed, her hair and makeup absolutely perfect, and she looked ready to make her big debut at Crescent Cove High today.

"And I've already reserved my ride with Eliza," said Taylor a bit too smugly. She too was perfection—at least on the surface. But DJ was well aware that looks can be deceiving.

Eliza smiled at DJ now. "And I told Kriti she could ride with me too … which only leaves room for one more." Eliza and DJ hadn't really spoken since last night when they'd made their splashy entrance into Harry's beach-house party together. A few hours and a lifetime later, DJ had left the party and driven all the girls (except Taylor and Eliza who weren't ready to go) back to the Carter House in her grandmother's car.

They barely made it home before curfew, and DJ felt certain that the party-hardy girls, Taylor and Eliza, got back quite a bit later than that. Although, as far as DJ knew, Mrs. Carter hadn't said a word.

Naturally, this double standard aggravated DJ. Not that it was unexpected since her grandmother clearly favored those two, but it did seem a bad omen for the year ahead. Still, DJ was determined not to complain. Because today was not only the first day of school, it was also the first day following DJ's amazing life-changing episode on the beach last night. And she didn't want to blow it by getting mad.

"School's not that far away," pointed out Rhiannon. "I don't mind walking. That's how I used to get there."

DJ had walked to school last year as well. And she wouldn't mind walking today, except that she had on a new pair of Michael Kors shoes — ones that Eliza had coaxed her to buy, telling her they would be perfect for the first day of school. Now DJ wondered if she should run upstairs and change them. Maybe she should change her whole outfit and go back to her old style of casual grunge sportswear. Although she knew that would upset her grandmother, not to mention Eliza.

"I will drive the other girls to school today," proclaimed Mrs. Carter with a loud sigh. DJ could tell that her grandmother was not pleased with this setup. Still, wasn't this her own fault for boarding this many girls? She should've considered there might be transportation problems down the line.

Eliza smiled at DJ now. "So, do you want to ride with us then?"

DJ glanced over at Casey and Rhiannon. These two still looked like the Carter House misfits, although at least Rhiannon was trying. Casey, on the other hand, could clearly not care less. DJ briefly considered abandoning them to ride with Eliza — in the cool car. And maybe she would've done just that yesterday. But today things were different. She was different. And so she simply shook her head. "No, that's okay, Eliza. I can ride with my grandmother today."

Eliza frowned. "Are you sure?"

"Yeah, but thanks anyway." DJ could tell that Eliza was not happy about her choice. And she suspected that Eliza had hoped to make a flashy entrance this morning, probably with Taylor on one side and DJ on the other—maybe with Kriti trailing slightly behind them like a handmaid. And, of course, Eliza probably hoped that Rhiannon and Casey, who did not measure up to her fastidious fashion standards, would lag somewhere far, far behind.

"Well, I'm going up to put on my finishing touches," said Eliza lightly. "And then I'll be ready." As if on cue, the breakfast table began to vacate. And before long, they were all on their way to school. The sporty white Porsche, with its three fashionable girls, drove about a block ahead, while Mrs. Carter's more sensible silver Mercedes followed discretely behind.

Rhiannon and Casey sat silently in the backseat, and DJ sat next to her grandmother, wondering what school would be like this year. Feeling nervous, she fidgeted with the handle of her Hermès bag. Of course, this only reminded her of that embarrassing moment at the beach when Taylor had used the contents in the purse to humiliate her. Still, it seemed that DJ and Conner had made it past that. It seemed that he had really liked her. And she knew she liked him. They'd even gone out since then. And after that, it seemed that their relationship had begun to unravel.

Still, she couldn't put her finger on what had gone wrong between them last night. Maybe she would never know. On one hand, she told herself that it might be for the best.

After all, she had just invited Jesus into her heart. Perhaps that was what she needed to focus on for the time being. And yet, she couldn't deny that she still really liked Conner. And she still wanted him to like her. She tried to block the disturbing image of him and Taylor dancing together last night. Or Taylor's superior expression this morning. Like she'd won. And she reminded herself that Conner had kissed her—before he'd said what sounded like a final good-bye. None of it made much sense. And thinking about it just frustrated her more.

DJ suddenly remembered what Rhiannon had told her before they'd gone to bed last night. "If you're stressing about something, just pray. There's actually a verse in the Bible that says to do this."

Well, DJ wasn't sure she really knew how to pray, but she *was* definitely stressing over Conner. And for that reason, as Mrs. Carter turned down the road to the school, DJ made a feeble attempt to pray. Naturally, she did this silently. No way was she going to start praying out loud with her critical grandmother and Casey, the rebel girl, listening in. She said the words silently inside her head. She just hoped that God could hear her, and that he was listening. And, by the time Mrs. Carter pulled in front of the school, DJ felt amazingly calm. Maybe this prayer thing really did work.

"Will you pick us up afterward?" asked DJ.

Her grandmother nodded. "At three?"

"That's about right," said DJ. "Although I have volleyball after school. And Kriti said she might try out too. In that case, everyone would fit in Eliza's car."

"Wouldn't that be delightful?!" Mrs. Carter seemed relieved now, and DJ suspected she was calculating how much afternoon naptime she was willing to sacrifice for the sake of the girls. "How about if you give me a call when you know for sure, Desiree?"

"Okay."

Mrs. Carter smiled and waved. "Have a nice day, girls."

Rhiannon politely thanked her, and DJ grabbed her gym bag and waved, but Casey just grunted as if this prospect of having a good day was highly unlikely.

Unfortunately, that would probably be the case with Casey. Going to Crescent Cove High dressed like Goth Girl meets Punk Rocker might not go over too well. Just this morning, DJ had tried to warn Casey of this, but the stubborn girl was not ready to listen to anyone. Still, it seemed a little unfair that DJ and Rhiannon were stuck walking into the building with Casey. It was her choice to stand out like a loser, but why did she have to subject them to it as well? Then, when DJ imagined what the three of them must look like together, she almost laughed. Almost. She just hoped, as they headed for the school's entrance, that others would have as much self-control. What a whacky threesome.

DJ, thanks to her grandmother's and Eliza's fashion intervention, looked fairly stylish. Although, according to Casey, DJ had simply been transformed into "an Eliza clone." Casey, in total contrast, with her safety-pin-pierced brows and skull T-shirt and black lace-up boots, looked freaky weird. This was aside from the fact that her hair—cut in a short Mohawk and dyed jet black with an electric-blue stripe down the middle—was a real show stopper. Then there was Rhiannon, who DJ thought actually looked sort of cool in her own unique design of "recycled" retro clothes and funky-junky jewelry. Unfortunately this was also a style that some of the snobby mean girls would be glad to take turns slamming. Yes, they were making quite an entrance.

205

"Hey, DJ," called Eliza from behind them.

DJ paused at the top of the steps and then turned to see Eliza, Taylor, and Kriti crossing the street from the student parking lot and casually strolling toward them. DJ waved and waited, but Casey just kept on walking into the school as if she was resolved to get this over with ASAP—not unlike a convicted murderer on her way to the electric chair. DJ actually called out, but Casey just kept on going, didn't even look back. Whatever.

"Here we go, girls," said Eliza with a smile. "Are we ready?"

DJ could feel them being watched as they entered the school. Even so, she held her head up high. Okay, maybe she was imitating Eliza now, but if it worked, what difference did it make? All DJ knew was that she didn't want to take the same abuse she'd suffered last spring.

"Where's the security?" asked Taylor.

"What?" said Rhiannon.

"You know, X-ray machines, gates, uniforms ... What's the deal?"

"We don't have them," said DJ.

"We're such a small town," explained Rhiannon. "I guess they don't think we need all that."

"That's one thing I won't miss," said Taylor as they continued down the hallway.

"I'm supposed to pick up my registration packet in the office," said Eliza. "Where is that?"

"Right this way," said DJ. "I have to pick up mine too."

As it turned out, they had all registered online, so they all needed to go to the office. Several of the kids from last night's party greeted the girls and, as they continued to the office, DJ began to relax a little. Maybe this wasn't going to be so bad after all. She tried not to worry about Casey, although she did feel concerned. But perhaps this was just something Casey needed to work through on her own—like a rite of passage. Not that DJ would wish that on anyone.

At the office, Mrs. Seibert, the counselor, welcomed them. Apparently she'd already heard about the Carter House girls and seemed curious as to how it was going. DJ gave her a quick summary, trying to play down the circus element of their living arrangements, and Mrs. Seibert handed them their registration packets. "We're a little short on lockers again this year. Do you girls mind doubling up?"

"Not at all," said Eliza. She turned quickly to DJ now. "Want to be locker partners?"

DJ could feel Taylor glaring at her as she nodded and muttered a meek, "Sure."

"And the rest of you?" asked Mrs. Seibert.

"I don't mind sharing," said Kriti.

"I'll share with her," offered Taylor without enthusiasm.

"I can share with Casey," said Rhiannon.

"Who's Casey?"

"Casey Atwood," offered DJ. "She's new too."

"Another Carter House girl?" asked Mrs. Seibert with raised brows.

"Yes."

Mrs. Seibert nodded. "Interesting."

"Yes," said Eliza. "It has been."

"So, do you girls need anyone besides Rhiannon to show you around the school?" asked Mrs. Seibert. "We do have some student guides."

"That's okay," said DJ. "I was actually here for a few weeks last year, so between the two of us, I think we can handle it."

"Well, I hope you'll all have a wonderful year at CCH."

"Thank you," said Eliza politely. "It seems like a very nice school."

Of course, this evoked a snide remark from Taylor. They were barely out of the office when she said something about the espresso shade of Eliza's nose. But Eliza just shrugged it off. "It never hurts to be nice, Taylor. Someday you may even figure that out for yourself."

Then Eliza sided up to DJ. "Looks like we have first period together, as well as some other classes. Want to show me around?"

"Sure."

Rhiannon fell into step with Taylor now. "I noticed we have some classes together too, Taylor. You need any directions?"

"I suppose that would be helpful," said Taylor in a bored and I'm-so-much-better-than-you tone.

"And we have our maps," said Kriti as she slipped a paper out of the folder. "I think I can find my way to the science department on my own. I have chemistry first period."

"Chemistry," said Taylor with a disgusted expression. "Why on earth would you intentionally subject yourself to *that?*"

"It's called education," said Kriti.

"It's called *boring*," said Taylor.

"Let's find our lockers first," suggested DJ.

"Like I'm going to use a locker," said Taylor with disgust.

"You mean you're going to carry everything around with you?" asked Rhiannon.

Taylor held up her oversized Burberry bag. "Why not?"

"What about when it's winter and you have coats and scarves and mittens and things?" persisted Rhiannon. "You're going to haul all that around with you too?"

Taylor seemed to consider this. "Maybe I'll look into the locker ..."

They quickly found their lockers. After several failed attempts at the combination lock, DJ finally let Eliza take a turn at opening the locker. Naturally, it opened on the first try. Eliza just laughed. "I guess I have the touch."

DJ threw her gym bag in and slammed the door shut.

"See you later," called Kriti. "I don't want to be late to chem class."

Taylor turned to Rhiannon now. "Lead me to the music department."

Rhiannon did a fake salute. "Yes, sir." And they took off.

"And the English department is this way," said DJ, pointing in the opposite direction.

"This is fun," said Eliza as they navigated through the crowded hallway.

"Fun?" echoed DJ.

"Sure ... all these new people, new challenges. Don't you think it's fun?"

DJ considered this. "Yeah, maybe. I guess I just hadn't looked at it like that before."

"Hey, there's Conner and Harry up ahead." Eliza waved and DJ cringed. She just wasn't ready for this yet. Still, there seemed no choice but to paste on a happy face and act as if all was well.

2

"Welcome to CCH," said Harry as he slipped an arm around Eliza's waist, "home of the Mighty Maroons."

"*Maroons*?" echoed Eliza. "As in the color maroon?"

"Well, it is our school color," said Harry. "But there's actually a story behind the word *maroon*."

"A story I don't have time to hear," said Conner. "Excuse me, ladies." Then he sort of nodded and dashed off.

"Conner doesn't want to be late on his first day of school," said Harry in a teasing tone. "Which way you girls heading anyway?"

"English," said DJ calmly. She was trying to act perfectly natural, as if Conner's quick departure wasn't really a rejection, as if it had nothing to do with her, and as if it hadn't hurt her feelings.

"So am I," said Harry happily.

"So what is the maroon story?" asked Eliza as the three of them continued toward the English department together.

"Well, maroon is for *marooned*, as in passengers who are dumped off a ship—apparently this used to happen with illegally gotten slaves. If the ship was being pursued by the law, the captain would dump the slaves on an island."

"And that's our mascot?" Eliza was clearly confused. "Like we're slaves who've been dumped here? Not too flattering."

"That's not the whole story. The marooned people turned out to be really feisty, and they fought for their freedom when the ship came back to get them."

"I guess that makes a little sense." Although Eliza didn't look fully convinced as they paused by Room 233.

Harry grinned. "Hey, I don't make this stuff up."

Eliza patted Harry on the cheek now. "Well, you are an awfully smart boy. I think I might like to keep you around."

Then he leaned over and gave her a little peck on the forehead. "Later." And he continued on down the hall.

"English lit, I presume?" asked Eliza as DJ headed into the classroom.

DJ nodded, pointing to a couple of seats in the back.

"No." Eliza put her hand on DJ's arm to stop her. Then, pointing to a pair of seats closer to the front, she leaned over and whispered. "Back-row seats are for losers or snoozers, dear."

DJ wasn't sure that she totally agreed with Eliza's little rhyme, but she followed her anyway. Who knew, maybe Eliza really had this all figured out. And maybe there were a few tricks that DJ could learn from this rather sophisticated girl. For starters, DJ would like to ask Eliza how one is supposed to deal with certain boys — the kind who liked you one day but not the next. Especially those particularly mysterious ones like Conner. Maybe she would ask her about this later.

DJ tried to pay attention as Mrs. Devin, a teacher who looked like she should've retired in the last millennium, droned on about what their lucky class would study this semester. It sounded like a fairly boring overview of the literary works of people who had been dead and buried for centuries. DJ couldn't even remember why she'd chosen this class in the first place — probably just to knock off one of her English requirements and make sure that she could still have PE for seventh period (since that always made it easier for after-school sports). But if today was any sign of what was to come, DJ probably would've been better off in the back row because she really did feel like snoozing right now.

Instead, she began to daydream about Conner. But her daydreams were more tormented than enjoyable. And because she felt seriously worried that everything was over between them, she decided to pray. It wasn't as if she thought she had God in her back pocket now, but she figured that he might be able to help her out some. At least she hoped so.

The morning continued uneventfully. In a way that was something to be grateful for. Last spring, DJ had desperately wished for uneventful. She had longed to simply disappear into the woodwork, but instead she had seemed to stand out like she had a flashing neon sign strapped to her chest that said, "Pick on the new girl." For some reason — maybe it was due to her makeover or Eliza's friendship — that no longer seemed to be the case.

Unfortunately for Casey, the mean girls still needed a target. DJ hadn't actually witnessed this yet, but right before fourth period, Taylor gave Eliza a detailed report. "You should've seen Casey's face," she told DJ, "when those girls — the self-appointed fashion police — started tearing into her about her wardrobe choices. Talk about brutal. I wasn't sure if Casey was going to give it back to them or run. As it turned out, she just stood there and took it." Naturally, DJ felt horrible for Casey, but perhaps the most disturbing thing was how Taylor seemed to enjoy relaying this pathetic little story.

"She actually got slammed up against the lockers then," said Taylor. "Hit her head and everything."

"That's terrible," said Eliza. "I hope she reported this."

Taylor laughed. "Yeah, right. Then those girls would probably really tear into her."

"Why did they do that?" demanded DJ.

Taylor rolled her eyes dramatically. "Why do you think they did that?"

"Because they're just plain mean," said Eliza.

"And because Casey is just plain begging for it," said Taylor. "You can't dress and act like that unless you want serious trouble. And she is definitely getting it."

"Poor Casey," said Eliza. "I wish we could do an intervention."

"A fashion intervention," said Taylor as the three of them went into US History together.

They'd barely sat down when Mr. Myers began taking roll. DJ tried not to worry about Casey, but Taylor's awful story of Casey slammed up against the lockers kept replaying through her mind. Despite the abuse DJ took last year, nothing like that had ever happened to her. Aside from the fact that it must be completely humiliating to be treated like that, what if this bullying continued or got worse? What if Casey got seriously hurt? Finally, DJ took Rhiannon's advice again. Instead of worrying obsessively about Casey, DJ prayed for her. She prayed that God would do an intervention. Maybe something like what had happened to her just last night. It was hard to believe that scene on the beach had occurred less than 24 hours ago. But she was thankful for it just the same.

After history, the girls headed to the commons. "Let's put our stuff on that table," instructed Eliza as they entered the commons. "Then we can get some lunch."

"If there's lunch worth getting." Taylor flopped her bag onto a chair and scowled. "I think I'll ask Clara to pack me a lunch tomorrow."

Then the three of them went over to get in the lunch line. Eliza spotted Kriti coming into the commons and waved to her, pointing out the table that they had just reserved. But just as Kriti was placing her bag on the round table, a couple of girls that DJ remembered from last year approached her. They pointed angrily at the table, and although DJ couldn't hear them, she could tell they were saying something mean.

"Look." DJ nudged Eliza then pointed toward the table. "I think those girls are giving Kriti a hard time."

"Why don't you go rescue our Indian princess," teased Taylor.

"Maybe I will," DJ shot back at her.

"I'll save your place," said Eliza.

DJ wished that Eliza had offered to accompany her instead, but she headed back to the table anyway.

"You don't look old enough to be in high school," said Madison Dormont to Kriti. This was one of the same girls who had picked on DJ last spring. "What are you, like twelve or something?"

"Maybe she's a child genius," teased the other girl, Tina Clark, another foul-mouthed mean girl.

"What's the matter?" said Madison. "No speakee English?"

"Is there a problem here?" demanded DJ from behind her.

Madison turned with narrowed eyes. Then she peered more closely as if trying to remember DJ. "Yeah, the problem is that this is *our* table."

DJ stood taller as she simply shook her head. "I don't think so."

"It is so," insisted Tina.

"Sorry, but it's *our* table now. My friends and I already put our stuff here." DJ pointed over to where Taylor and Eliza were waiting in line and watching rather intently. "See," she said as if speaking to very young children, "those are *my* friends and these are *our* bags and this is *our* table."

Madison and Tina both looked over at the lunch line now. Just then Eliza smiled and cupped her hand in a cute little wave and Taylor waved too, although not nearly as sweetly, and her expression was totally serious and somewhat intimidating.

"Whatever!" snapped Madison. "But just because you and your Barbie-doll friends got this table today, doesn't mean you'll get it next time."

"I guess we'll see about that," said DJ.

Then she and Kriti watched as the intruders went to save another table. DJ turned to Kriti, who still looked a little upset. "Those girls are so lame." DJ shook her head. "Why don't I stay with our things for now." Then she dug a five-dollar bill out of her purse and handed it to Kriti. "Just order me a cheeseburger and fries and a coke, okay?"

Kriti nodded with an uncertain expression.

"Eliza will give you cuts in line," promised DJ.

"Okay." Kriti went over and DJ sat down, ready to ward off any more interlopers.

Before long, Rhiannon showed up. DJ told her to leave her stuff and go get some lunch. "Did you see Casey?" she asked as Rhiannon hung the strap of her large carpet bag over the back of a chair.

"Not since third period. I have art with her."

"How did she seem then?"

Rhiannon's brow creased. "Not happy."

DJ kept an eye out for Casey, but she didn't see her any-where in the commons. DJ wondered what she'd do if she did see her. Would she invite her to join them? And if she did, would the others get mad? Not Rhiannon, of course, but Taylor would. And Eliza might not show it, but she'd be irritated too. Maybe Casey had made some new friends by now—freaky kids who needed to make a statement to the world by making themselves look ridiculous.

Finally, Eliza, Taylor, and Kriti came back to the table, setting down their lunches and getting seated.

"I can't believe you're going to eat that." Taylor eyed DJ's cheeseburger with undisguised disgust. "Do you have any idea how many calories are in that greasy meal?"

"Fat too," warned Eliza. "You really should be more careful, DJ."

"Thanks for the nutritional counseling session," said DJ. "But don't worry, I'll burn off all the calories and more at volleyball practice after school."

"You are seriously going out for volleyball?" asked Taylor.

"Well, it's not that serious, but I am going out."

"You actually want to hang with the jock girls and go around smelling like Deep Heat and old sweat socks?"

DJ made a face at Taylor before taking a big a bite of her cheeseburger.

"Just when I thought there was hope for you." Taylor turned to Eliza now. "See, you can take the grunge outta that girl, but you can't take the girl outta the grunge."

"Volleyball is fun," insisted DJ. "And good exercise." She pointed a fry at the salads that Eliza, Taylor, and Kriti were picking at. "And if you guys went out for sports, you could indulge in some real food instead of grazing on greens all the time."

DJ looked at Kriti now. "And what about you? You mentioned that you'd think about going out?"

Kriti's brow creased. "I don't think so."

"But you're good."

217

She nodded. "Yes, but I'm considering something else."

"What?" demanded DJ.

Kriti looked down at her salad and mumbled, "Debate team."

"Hello, geek squad," said Taylor.

"My forensics teacher thinks I'd be good. He's already encouraging me to try out for it."

"Why wouldn't he?" said Taylor. "I'm sure it's not easy to recruit kids, even the geeks, enticing them to put on those shapeless debate team jackets and stand in front of a live audience and make total fools of themselves."

Kriti scowled at Taylor now. "I wonder what you'll be saying ten years from now, Taylor, when I am an attorney or maybe even a judge and you're serving cocktails in an airport lounge."

Taylor laughed. "Yeah, right."

Eliza lifted her hand in a big wave now, and DJ looked up in time to see Harry and Conner strolling their way. Harry was smiling, but Conner looked as if he was seeking another quick escape route. And this just made DJ just plain mad. She knew it was because of her, but she didn't know why. And if Conner was this uncomfortable with her, maybe he should just get it out in the open. This whole avoidance, running away, and hiding from her business was getting beyond ridiculous. Good grief, the way Conner was acting, you'd think she had some contagious disease or cooties or something. What was wrong with the boy?

"Maybe I should just leave," she said quietly to Eliza.

Eliza turned and looked at her. "Why?"

"Because Conner obviously has a problem with me," she whispered.

Then Eliza sort of nodded. "Now that you mention it, I did notice that you two seemed to be at odds last night."

Taylor laughed loudly. "At odds? Don't you get it, Eliza? Conner just isn't into DJ anymore. Isn't that obvious?"

Naturally, Taylor made this flattering statement when the guys were close enough to overhear her. Humiliated once again by Taylor, DJ looked down at her barely touched, calorie-laden cheeseburger and fries, which suddenly looked totally unappetizing. But that might've had to do with the rock that she felt lodged in her stomach just then. So, scooping up her Hermès bag and unfinished soda, she quickly stood. "Excuse me," she said, without looking up. She didn't want to see Conner's face. Face burning, she turned and walked straight toward the door. Look who was running now.

Carter House Girls Series from Melody Carlson

Mix six teenage girls and one '60s fashion icon (retired, of course) in an old Victorian-era boarding home. Add boys and dating, a little high school angst, and throw in a Kate Spade bag or two ... and you've got the Carter House Girls, Melody Carlson's new chick lit series for young adults!

Mixed Bags
Book One

Stealing Bradford
Book Two

Homecoming Queen
Book Three

Viva Vermont!
Book Four

Lost in Las Vegas
Book Five

New York Debut
Book Six

Spring Breakdown
Book Seven

Last Dance
Book Eight

Available in stores and online!

On the Runway Series
from Melody Carlson

When Paige and Erin Forrester are offered their own TV show, sisterly bonds are tested as the girls learn that it takes two to keep their once-in-a-lifetime project afloat.

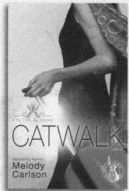

Premiere
Book One

Catwalk
Book Two

Rendezvous
Book Three

Spotlight
Book Four

Glamour
Book Five

Ciao
Book Six

Available in stores and online!

Sweet Seasons
by Debbie Viguié!

Join Candace Thompson on a sweet, lighthearted, and honest romp through the friendships, romances, family and friend dramas, and faith discoveries that make a girl's life as full as it can be.

Summer of Cotton Candy
Softcover: 978-0-310-71558-0

Fall of Candy Corn
Softcover: 978-0-310-71559-7

Winter of Candy Canes
Softcover: 978-0-310-71752-2

Spring of Candy Apples
Softcover: 978-0-310-71753-9

Also available in ebook versions.

Available in stores and online!

Visit www.zondervan.com/teen

Real Life Series
from Nancy Rue

Four girls are brought together through the power of a mysterious book that helps them sort through the issues of their very real lives.

Motorcycles, Sushi and One Strange Book
Softcover: 978-0-310-71484-2

Boyfriends, Burritos and an Ocean of Trouble
Softcover: 978-0-310-71485-9

Tournaments, Cocoa and One Wrong Move
Softcover: 978-0-310-71486-6

Limos, Lattes & My Life on the Fringe
Softcover: 978-0-310-71487-3

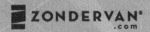